Hunted

Joseph Daniels

[2015]

1

My bed felt amazing. My duvet was wrapped around under my chin, my muscles felt relaxed and my warm pillow fitted snugly under my head. But the gash of golden sunlight leaking between my silk curtains was tormenting me.

I didn't have the guts to crane my neck and look at my flashing bedside clock, but I knew I had to shift myself out of bed. In less than two hours I would have my elbows propped up on a polished, circular table discussing business and boring statistics with a bunch of yawning old dullards.

Today was going to be worse than normal because my Marketing Director, Jayne Howard would give me a lecture for a few hours about how I had not filed my monthly report and about how badly I was failing.

I guess that's what I get for being a billionaire, genius scientist who revolutionised the world in Science and Technology.

Five years ago I had become a world famous phenomenon, known worldwide. My name 'Joey Tyler' was featured in every science magazine and every techie show ever. Whilst my face was printed on billboards worldwide, with my *slogan,* 'Think further'. I had created bionic livers for heavy drinkers, cars that worked by a simple voice command and even 14 automated towers, positioned across The world, fully manned by a hard-working group of androids, building my inventions and shipping them worldwide. Each tower had only two human employees except for the one in London which was fully staffed by people; geniuses from across the world.

Then I had decided to create the first ever manned mission to Mars, a 12 man group hand - picked by me and sent to the red planet. Everything in the two years of building ran smoothly, the rocket was made to perfection, six men and six women were specially trained. Everything was going great.

2

On The 11th of July 2010 the rocket was set to launch, the world was in awe as these people did what no one had ever done before. The rocket launched, everyone cheered, the rocket hit the atmosphere and blew up, twelve deaths enough rocket fuel in the sky to hugely accelerate Global Warming. All eyes turned to me, news reporters said that I was unfit to even be a Scientist, families of the dead astronauts created petitions to have me fired.

Then I was fired.

My company W.S.I (World Science Innovations) fired me leaving me here in a 12 million pound mansion; just here doing nothing.

Then after two months they realised that I was a crucial part of the Company, so I continued to work for them; in secret.

I didn't like working for them, W.S.I was a Trillion pound industry but it was hugely corrupt, its founder, Spanish Billionaire Rico Angel, would do anything to turn over a profit from shipping immigrants into the country to selling dodgy guns to dodgy teenagers at exceedingly high prices. On several occasions I had built something that I thought was helping people then was transformed into something for killing people. I had no other choice, W.S.I owned the deeds to my house and if I quit I would be left homeless. Life had been a lot easier when I was working for N.A.S.A.

I hadn't been shouted at everyday then.

Now half of my projects were helping the world and the other half bringing it even closer to destruction.

Months ago I had created a new form of Rocket Propelled Grenade with triple the power of a standard RPG. The British army stormed into a Saudi Arabian village with them and not one shot was fired before the people they were hunting down surrendered. Unfortunately a group of Malaysian terrorists managed to intercept a crate full of them and killed 54 people in the same month.

Ninety five percent of W.S.I staff were completely in the dark about their companies dodgy dealings, some had suspicions of conspiracies, but none of them knew that their wages came from drug dealing, human trafficking and illegal firearms selling. The more

4

Rico's staff was in the dark the better it would be, for everyone's sakes.

The only reason I was still alive was because of the fact that I had never told a soul about what happened at my job, except for Sam. If I ever did tell anyone then I would soon become a bloated corpse in The Atlantic Ocean.

"Didn't you hear me; get out of bed you lazy sod!" Suddenly I snapped awake, shooting up. My silk curtains flew apart, exposing completely me to the warm glow and golden rays.

Blearily I tried to burrow my way under my covers but it was too late. My winter duvet was yanked off of me. I tried to fight back, ramming my head under my soft pillow to bury all thoughts of the harsh reality of the meeting I was potentially already late for.

Unfortunately the person trying to get me out of bed was a green belt in Karate, Kung Fu and Tiquando. This meant an almighty shove sent me rolling off of my bed and sprawled out onto a carpet, that I noticed face down, desperately need vacuuming.

My best friend, Sam, loomed over me, the evil grin plastered on his face that he always got when he had knocked me down or had beaten me at something that wasn't Chess, like he always did. Although I was academically gifted, when it came to sport that wasn't on the Wii I wasn't the best.

"Get off your bum," snapped Sam. "It's already 9:20!" As it dawned on me that I had to leave in less than two minutes I instantly sprang up. Like a bullet I shot down the landing, pushing Sam out of the way and bounded down stairs that never seemed to end. As I jumped over the banisters I realised I was wearing nothing but a pair of white boxers and the blue crystal locket I had inherited from my parents.

I made a sudden U-turn and heading towards my walk in wardrobe. I picked a slice of Pepperoni Pizza from the night before off of my antique table from Henry VIII's castle.

Panting I collapsed into my dressing room then tore the place apart looking for my 'business suit'.

After a minute of frantic searching I dashed out of the room wearing crumpled trousers, a creased white shirt with only half of the buttons done up and a tie I had just left hanging around my neck.

I charged past Sam again on the landing, he just shrugged and strode after me. Leaping down the stairs, three steps at a time, I desperately tried to do up my tie. At the bottom of the stairs I slipped my feet into a pair of battered blue vans without any socks, I looked ridiculous wearing a business suit and casual plimsolls, yet I didn't care. I should because I was on thin ice at W.S.I, but I didn't. I opened the front door and slipped across a dew-soaked lawn towards my blue Lamborghini parked at the end of the garden. Slamming into the side of the car, my heart was racing two hundred beats per minutes. I fumbled in my Jacket pockets, probing for my car keys which I realised despondently weren't there. In frustration I hammered my fists against the car door.

"Looking for these?" said Sam from the doorway with a devilish grin; incongruous with his angelic features made up of Blonde, curly hair, glistening blue eyes. His clothes looked neat, a white polo shirt white chinos and white socks, later they wouldn't be. Sam spent his days

7

pigged out on my sofa watching re-runs of 'Friends'

He had my car keys spinning around his index finger.

"Give 'em here you moron," I ordered

"Whatever," shrugged Sam and in one swift movement the keys flew across the air and I grasped them in my palm. I didn't thank Sam, just jammed the keys into the door and flung it open.

Once in the driver's seat I turned the ignition key and slammed my foot down on the accelerator as far down as it would go. The blue beast of my car did nothing, just shuddered and spluttered. I put the gear stick into the right position so that the Lamborghini sprung to life and shot down the road at speed. Right now I didn't care about seatbelts or speeding tickets, I just had to get to work on time.

I sped down the long stretch of road parallel to my house; sending a flurry of autumn leaves into the air as I zoomed past. Until after a few minutes until I saw the familiar patch of forest to my left. Slowing down I turned towards the unmade road that lead into the woods; at the end of which was a small wooden hut.

As I neared I tapped on miniscule red button underneath my dashboard that caused the hut to open up and split in half, the wood cracking as it revealed a dark slope heading underground. I drove onto the slope into a wide tunnel that went deep underneath London; below The Tube.

It was a wide cavern Rico often referred to as Smuggler's Tunnel. It linked The W.S.I building with many places across the country, drugs, guns and people often were transported through here. Rico had set up environmental conservation acts so that no one was allowed to dig above the tunnels including the government, who were completely blind to this area. I had to use this tunnel so that I was not seen working for W.S.I.

I sped along the dimly lit tunnel, straight at a rock wall, my finger pushed down on the red button again and the wall hissed open revealing an underground car park. I was now in the sub-levels of W.S.I's London building, this was floor zero and I had to get to floor 154 in one minutes.

I parked between two black SUVs, jumped out of the car and sprinted towards the elevator.

Then I pressed the button and thankfully the metal doors opened straight away. I hastily pressed button 154 and when the elevator asked for ID I slid my Passcard over a scanner imbedded in the wall. The doors shut with a clang, anxiously I watched the floor numbers. 1, 2, 3, 4, 5, 6, 7, 7, 7. The Elevator was taunting me, trying to make me even later than I would already be.

"Come on!" I shouted then the elevator moved again 8, 9, 10. The wait was agonising, I was mildly claustrophobic and today I had even more of a reason to get out of this enclosed metal box.

"Come on!" I screamed at, somehow I found myself kicking the side; it wasn't making anything happen other than hurting my toes.

Then the elevator shuddered and shot up at rocket speed, I had created this elevator to make getting between floors a lot easier.

151, 152, 153, 154. Finally!

I raged as the door slid open at snails speed, then as soon as there was enough space I squeezed between the doors and bolted towards the conference room like an angered Rhino.

The nine people sat silently and awkwardly around the table, waiting for the tenth person to enter the room and take his seat.

I burst through the door, dropping into my designated seat, as red as a tomato. Nine sets of scowling eyes fell upon me as I rested my elbows on the table. Jayne Howard stared at me.

"Where have you been?" she demanded, acid in her voice.

"Asleep," I choked, not caring how badly she would blast at me later.

"And where is your report?" she snapped like an Ice Queen.

I scanned the room then noticed who was sitting at the end of the table, there staring down at me with evil in his eyes sat Rico Angel. His fingers intertwined, tapping against each other in rhythm, a sign that he was impatient. I noticed small specks of blood on his collar.

"Welcome, Mister Tyler," snarled Rico. "We're here to discuss your, *contract*."

2

"Please sit," said Rico with his best fake smile. This was a very strange comment as I was already sat down comfortably.   "Morning sir," I yawned, purposely showing no interest, resting my feet up on the table.

"We need to talk," wheezed Rico, his face was friendly and warm, but I could see through the ruse.

Around him everyone had very different expressions; some were feeling sorry for me whilst others were delighted at the thought I might be leaving.

"About what sir?" I said. Something clicked inside Rico and his happy nature dispersed into the air leaving behind his usual persona.

"Get your filthy feet off of my table or you will live to regret it!" snarled Rico. "Or you won't live."

The sudden outburst shocked me and I fell off of the table onto a heap on the polished glass floor. I had a perfect view of the lab below, men and woman in white lab coats bustled about, brewing concoctions and mixing chemicals.

A small ginger man carrying a briefcase trudged out of the room below, his briefcase hanging open, as a stained old document fluttered out of it. A scientist behind picked it up the document but instead of returning it to its owner he walked off with it. The ginger man entered the elevator and I noticed a drop of blood fall from his hand. Whilst I was transfixed on the scene below Jayne's voice broke my concentration as she shouted.

"Didn't you hear me?" screeched Jayne in her shrill voice. "Get off the floor you oaf!"

I picked myself up and dropped down on the chair, smiling at Jayne with a small, smirk.

"What's your problem?" I scolded.

"Her problem is our, breach in security," snapped Rico. "Some people here tipped off The Serious Organised Crime Agency and the government have been on my arse all night."

"So I'm here, why?" I asked.

"One of The traitors was a young lad on the 72nd

floor," smiled Rico. "There's a bullet in him obviously."

"So you want me to find the other guy?" I said.

"We've already found him, actually," spat Jayne.

"I can talk for myself Jayne," said Rico, he then turned towards me. "We think it's you Mister Tyler."   "What!" I stuttered, never expecting Rico to blame me. "I have never betrayed you and never will."
"Get out!" shouted Rico, in a mad scramble dashed out of the room. Rico reached below his seat then pulled out a pistol. "I'm not going to shoot you, someone else will!" "Good luck Tyler," Rico called after me.

Looking behind me I slammed straight into the elevator, frantically I tapped the button repeatedly.

As if I would betray my company. I should have done it there and then. What was stopping me? Only deaths threat, the fact that Rico knew where I lived, he owned my house and had enough money to pay any government official to overlook my disappearance.

The elevator doors dinged open and I stormed in with so much rage that I didn't notice the man slouched in the corner at first. The ginger man I had seen underneath our meeting was slumped in the corner; blood flowed from the man and swirled around on the polished tiles of the elevator. The man's briefcase was stained red with his own blood. The man was unmoving, probably dead. I approached him and his head snapped up, his face was as pale as snow, and the only colour on him was the scarlet blood staining his clothes. His eyes were red-rimmed and extremely tired.

"Help me," he croaked, the man held up his left hand, the part of his body most stained by blood. He was missing his smallest finger; the stump was pumping out more blood than it should be.

"Who did this?" I asked.

"Rico," sobbed the man.

"Obviously," I muttered. "But why did he do that."   "He wanted the script. I wouldn't give him the script so he hurt me, I still didn't give him the script. But now he has the script and I have failed," rambled the man.

"What Script?"

"I found it on an archaeological dig in Cairo, Rico wanted it, said it was for The Ignotis," sobbed the man.

Before I could ask any more questions the elevator doors hissed open, revealing two mountainous men. Both wore the black and blue W.S.I security uniform, complete with a belt of pistols, batons and pepper sprays. The elite members of the force on the higher floors carried sub-machine guns.

"Mr Tyler," grunted the one on the left.

"Come with us." He gripped his huge sausage fingers around my forearm. He yanked me out into the lobby.

"You get the ginger one," barked the man holding me. The other man towered over the ginger man in the elevator.

I was frog-marched into the lobby, my arm painfully pressed between my shoulder blades. He held a BB gun to my back that was supposed to look like a real gun; I could see that his weapon was plastic however.

The man from the elevator shot past me, a sudden jolt of life in him.

"I've got him!" shouted the man holding me then he let loose a round of pellets into the fleeing man's back. The plastic balls hit his back with a crunch, knocking the ginger escapee through the revolving doors. The glass shattered into a million pieces. The noise silenced everyone in the lobby from tourists to employees.

In the momentary lapse I made a break for it, diving over the counter where a blonde receptionist screamed in shock. Two shots fired out of The BB gun so I pulled down the receptionist as small, plastic balls skimmed her head.

"Thanks," she spluttered but I was already leaping away behind a table. Everyone had taken cover under tables and behind desks. The ginger man was being dragged out of the glass which was raking up his arms, cutting them open.

"I've got one of them!" barked the guard into his radio on his shoulder as he dragged the unconscious bleeding man away. He hefted the

17

body into the elevator, nodding at his colleague, leaving him to deal with me.

"Come out Tyler," bellowed the man, firing a shot into the air so plaster fell around him. "Come out!"

"He's over here," screamed a Japanese tourist, her camera flapping around her neck.

"Bitch," I whispered and dived through my attacker's legs, I slipped forward thinking I would make it until he grabbed my collar, ripping me off of the floor and flailing me in front of him.

"Rico wants you upstairs," The butch mountain growled. Shaking me like a ragdoll. The receptionist I had rescued crept up behind the guard, raised a chair and smacked it down on his skull. The man grunted, shook on the spot for a few seconds then collapsed. I rolled out of the way before the hulking figure crushed me. Bounding away, and giving the receptionist a brief smile I then ran towards the stairs down to the car park; taking the steps five at a time. My wrecked, inappropriate shoes slapped against the wet concrete towards my Lamborghini.

As I leapt into the car five guards, with real guns, charged down the stairs, firing lead at me but completely missing me and my vehicle.

The car screeched as it spun around then leapt at the stone wall. The five men momentarily stopped, shocked at my stupidity. They were even more shocked when the wall split in two revealing a dark tunnel. Their slight confusion was a window of opportunity for me as I floored the accelerator, once again the car shuddered. I switched the gear then fired off leaving the men in a cloud of dust. I was propelled down the tunnel into the vast darkness like a blue bolt of lightning. Flicking a switch on the dashboard my headlamps flashed on revealing a forklift carrying a crate, I spun the steering wheel 180 degrees as the car swerved around the driver whose startled face stared at me with incredulity.

The car shifted sideways then fired back off into the tunnel.

In my rear view window I spotted two sleek, black Land Rovers with the yellow letters W.S.I spray-painted on the door.

I slammed my foot down again and left the cars behind, but my victory was short lived as the men shot forward within ten metres of me.

Underneath my radio was a built in phone which I opened by ordering, "Phone." The phone opened up, clearly displaying applications I might want to use.

"Call Sam," I demanded and the phone started dialling my best friends' number. The phone rang three times before Sam picked up. "S'up Joey," yawned Sam from my couch.

"Sam, help me Rico's trying to kill me!" I shouted at the car.

"You sure bro?" slurred Sam with a mouthful of pizza. "You're probably." Before I heard the rest of my friend's sentence I lost all signal and the car flew out of the tunnel through the woods. My Lamborghini crashed onto the road and skidded away, taking a shortcut off of the road. Soon my house was now in clear view.

Turning my head I realised that I was no longer being followed, with a sigh of relief I turned back and hit one of the palm trees in my garden at 80mph. My chest shone blue as I saw blonde hair approach.

3

Sam dropped me onto my unmade bed and trooped down the stairs. He strode past the swimming pool, into the living room. He approached the 80 inch Ultra HD TV and popped season ten of family guy into The Blu-Ray player.

Then as the DVD loaded he went into the kitchen and pulled a can of fosters from the fridge. He needed refreshment after lugging me up two sets of stairs. I had been in a car crash but after assessing me Sam ascertained I had no obvious physical so carried my unconscious body upstairs to regain consciousness. Sam wasn't too concerned for me; he thought I was probably drunk. As first I had rung him up, raving about Rico trying to kill him and then I had crashed right into the front garden.

I had form because two years ago I had got drunk and depressed so decided to go clubbing, a week later I was found in Italy. Sam couldn't judge me, I wasn't a heavy drinker but if I went clubbing or out to a party I would drink too much and not remember anything.

Sam dropped onto the huge white sofa/bed happily humming *'I love rock and roll'*. He took a swig from his fosters as the opening titles of *Family Guy* came on. There was nothing Sam loved more than laying in front of the TV; other than maybe swimming in my heated mineral. Just as Sam took a swig from his can, he heard a noise. Sets of footsteps from a few rooms away, they hadn't entered through the front door so they must have entered through the back door by the pool. So why hadn't the silent alarm alerted him? I had the alarm in my room, but I was in a deep sleep.

So Sam was alone with his mediocre martial arts skills. Maybe the intruders weren't attackers he thought to himself. The gun shot snapping over his head confirmed that they were. The wall exploded behind Sam as he dashed out of the room.

"I got him," barked one of the intruders. "You find the other guy, start downstairs."

He pulled the trigger on his shotgun and a barrage of buckshot punched tiny holes into the leather sofa.

Sam bounded through door after door, no idea where in the vast house he was headed, the direction he was going was towards the back door near the swimming pool.

Sam crashed into a door flinging it open, he was now inside my private spa pool room, this was a giant underground cavern filled with an Olympic-sized swimming pool. The blue water was completely still and mirror-like, depicting a calmness that as this moment Sam didn't feel. A small twisty slide and diving boards leading into the pool sat on the side.

"Get here you!" screamed Sam's attacker, firing lead balls that hit the top of the water, sending out small shockwaves of ripples destroying the calm surface.

To avoid being shot at again Sam dived straight into the pool, the refreshing water swirled around him, soaking his clothes and increasing his weight. With powerful strokes Sam sliced through the pool, propelling himself forward.

He was a strong swimmer but the man who had just gracefully dived into the pool was better, he advanced at Sam, making a grab for his ankle. Sam swerved away, spinning, and then he kicked the man in his square nose, swam to the side and pulled himself out of the pool.

He ran up plush, carpeted stairs, dripping water everywhere.

Sam ran into what used to be a Sushi bar whose use had been short lived after realising neither of us liked raw fish. On The cutting table lay a large fish knife, he eagerly snatched it up, running out of the room he made his way up the second set of stairs towards the bedroom landing.

As he drew closer to my room Sam saw that one of the three attackers stood outside my door. He hadn't seen Sam yet because he was busy looking down loading his sub-machine gun. A warm blue glow shone from under my door along with inaudible conversation.

As the man turned to open my bedroom door Sam dived forward, slashing his knife across the air. He wrapped his arm around the man's bulky neck; they both of them flew forward through my door revealing a stranger, his skin glowing fluorescent blue.

<u>4</u>

The glow was blue, not dark like Rico's heart but light and playful. It was a soft aquamarine that danced around in the sunlight.

25

No, it seemed more vibrant, like an electric blue. It was shifting, now it was a darker turquoise, very lively.

Wait, it was cyan, a light peaceful cyan. But where was it coming from, the light wasn't a reflection. Something was beaming the light up onto the ceiling. Me.

A pillar of thin blue light swirled up from my chest, seeping into the cracks and crevices of the ceiling, gently caressing them; blue tendrils snaked out of the light, flitting across the ceiling with a magical aura around it.

Slowly, I looked down the light was clearing filtering out of my locket.

Then the room span, it felt like someone had put my brain in a washing machine, my eyes rolled back in my head and my vision went blurry, yet I stayed conscious.

Inside me my vital organs jumped about, my stomach lurching, releasing thin sickly bile over my bedspread.

The smell, however, had no effect on me because I lost most sensation at that moment. My mouth felt dry, my nose wasn't filled with scents, and I could hear nothing. Nevertheless none of this was worse than the fact that I could not move. I lay paralyzed, unable to move a muscle, trapped under my sticky sheets.

Tension grew inside my chest as something tried to break free from my ribcage. The pain was unbearable and I would have done anything to make it stop, if I could have done anything.

Sweat flooded over me as my temperature somersaulted upwards, spasms stretched across me flicking my limbs painfully up and down.

The blood pulsing through me bubbled, threatening to burst any second. Eyes roll, teeth cracking, brain splitting. This could not get any worse. Then the head emerged from my chest.

The face, perfectly carved. Messy blonde hair precisely placed on his scalp. His eyes were closed, little creases around his brow, showing an expression of perfect serenity. The face was childlike, happy and innocent, yet it was obviously the face of a man in his twenties.

For a minute the pain shrank away, I managed a sigh of relief as I watched the most fascinating and most traumatising event of my life.

There was no gaping wound in my chest, no hole for the body to rise out of, the head just slipped up, with a pale blue glow emanating from his skull. The head still rose revealing a small mouth, pursed shut with a slight smirk. As the head and neck were revealed I noticed to ugly white bumps rising, each one foot from either side of the head, they were round and bony, rising up with the neck. Then came two slabs of shoulder, connecting the bumps to the neck.

Still the boy floated upwards. A muscular chest glided from me, followed by a torso, some parts I would prefer not to mention and then long slender legs.

The boy stayed still, held in the air by an invisible force drooping in the grip of a hand that I could not see.

Time froze for a second, the boy stayed in place; I could hear shouts in the distance. They weren't here; the shouts were outside a bubble enclosing me. The only sounds near me were my own heavy panting, as I tried to gasp in precious air whilst sweat drenched me.

I managed to sneak a glance towards my chest, fearing the worst, yet my fears were not confirmed. There was no sign that a 6ft man had squeezed out of my ribs.

"What are you?" I asked, the words barely escaping my lips. Suddenly there came a crack. A bolt of blue, electricity, fired from the boys head, bounced off of the ceiling, shooting down into the boy. The bolt went down the boy, radiating his skin with warm blue light. He seemed serene, until something inside him hissed and he let out a bellowing scream. The boy's back arch, his spine creaked and arms were bent at irregular angles. He started gurgling, a strange animal noise rumbling from his windpipe. The boy's eyelids snapped opened, they stared at me intensely.

"Hi Joey," smiled the boy.

I didn't know if it was exhaustion or pure shock but at that moment I passed out onto my sticky mattress.

When I awoke the boy was standing over me, staring at me as if I was a complete stranger. Which I was. I noticed he was no longer naked; he was wearing a Manchester United shirt signed by Cristiano Ronaldo that was too large for me and Nike shorts which he had pulled from my wardrobe.

"Good sleep?" asked the boy. "You've only been asleep for two minutes and four seconds."

"What happened?" I snapped. "Who are you? Where did you come from? How did you rise from my chest?" The sudden outburst left me short for breath for a few seconds. I was panicking, confused at the events of today. I had received a death threat from Rico and now this. They couldn't be linked. Could They?

"So many questions," huffed the boy in a voice full of serenity. "So little time." He then linked his index finger and thumb on each hand, forming a meditating pose.

"Answer me," I threatened, attempting to push my cover away but ending up tangled in the sticky sheets. Lewis grabbed the sheet then in a blur he threw it at the wall. It hit it with a sticky squelch and collapsed to the ground.

"No time because you are in danger Joey," explained the boy. "You are in serious danger. You and Sam." I shot up, squaring up to the boy who pushed me back."

"How are me and Sam in danger," I growled.

At that point Sam and a bulky man crashed through the door, reducing it to splinters. Sam waved a knife around the man but never actually stabbed him.

"Back Joey," ordered the boy, pushing me back, his skin glowing a weak blue.

5

"Die you bastard!" screamed Sam, waving the blade around the man's square head. The bulky man grabbed Sam then threw him forward into me. The two of us collided, hitting the wall.

"Hi mate," gasped Sam as we untangled ourselves from each other and the bed sheets.

The boy glided across the carpet and snatched the knife from Sam, his skin glowing an angry blue. He skidded forward with the grace of a ballerina but the ferocity of a lion. The boy then leapt into the air pirouetting round, landing by the bulky man. The blade sunk deep into the man's neck muscle. An unnatural gurgling sound resonated from our attacker's throat as a waterfall of blood slipped over his bottom lip. A pillar of scarlet squirted from the injured man's jugular vein soaking the boy, who yanked the knife from the bloody throat and kicked the body onto the floor. The corpse lay collapsed on the floor in a growing pool of his own blood.

Sam waddled over to the body, his face a mask of pale horror.

The boy skin had reverted back to its natural white colour, his face expressionless. The only evidence of the slaughter he had just committed was the blood splattered over his shirt that was thankfully already white.

On The man's shoulder a radio buzzed. *"Sergio."* grunted a man on the other radio. *"Sergio, what's happening up there?"*

Sam picked up the radio and held it to his ear.

"We're coming for you," buzzed the man through the radio. Sam dropped the radio and looked at me.

"We are in some pretty deep stuff now Joe," he said.

"We will get out," I reassured even though I was doubting our chances of surviving.

"The three of us will survive," barked the boy, punching his fist into the air.

"Who are you?" questioned Sam.

"I'm the guy who saved you," smiled the boy. Sam and I both stared at him. "Since that isn't good enough for you people, I'm Lewis."

At that moment, a round of bullets pounded the ornate ceiling, smashing holes into the crystal chandelier. Small sparkling shards rained over the room but Lewis had already gripped me and Sam, flinging us out of the door.

At the bottom of the stairs, one with a sniper rifle and the other with a sub-machine gun stood two men firing shots up.

On The man's sniper rifle, stencilled in gold block letters, was the name Xavier. The other man was nearly seven foot tall and I recognised him. He was Rico's nephew, Alonzo Angel; his father had been butchered so Rico had treated him like the son he had never had, using him as a wall to crush anyone who stood in his way.

Xavier squeezed the trigger on his sniper rifle, firing a five millimetre bullet up the staircase; it zoomed up splintering the banisters that we were crouched behind.

34

"How the hell do we get out Then, *Lewis*?" barked Sam, a rifle bullet whizzed over is messy flop of hair. He was still wet from his dip in the pool.

Alive," Lewis shouted. "I hope." He grabbed one of the only standing bits of the banister and pivoted himself over. Lewis fell faster than I thought humanly possible, landing gracefully on the ground. If anyone else had made that jump they would have broken their legs, but apparently not Lewis.

He jogged forward as Xavier swivelled round, trying to knock over Lewis with the butt of his huge gun. Lewis ducked under the barrel, slamming a fist into Xavier's ribcage. The Spanish bodyguard of Rico's let out a gasp, all air escaping his lungs as he doubled over. Lewis then brought a powerful chop onto the back of his throat. There was a crunch as Xavier flipped forward. Lewis snatched up the huge sniper rifle then without warning he cracked it down onto the winded Xavier's skull. Frankly I would have used the gun to shoot, what it's supposed to be used for.

"What a moron," I said as Lewis charged around Alonzo, into the kitchen. Lewis ran out of or sight, closely followed by the rhino that was Alonzo.

"Now's our chance," hissed Sam, he gripped my wrist and dragged me down the bullet riddled stairs. We tumbled down, heading towards the door for our escape. I didn't know Lewis and I would not die going back for him.

One step left, I lunged for the door handle as an iron grip clutched my ankle, bringing me down. I turned on the carpet to Xavier's mad grin, blood running between his teeth.

"Where you going Tyler?" he growled. I crawled away, rolled at the door but my efforts were useless because Xavier had stood up and grabbed my shirt. From his belt he drew a long jagged knife that looked like it had been used many times. "I'm going to gut you." growled Xavier, looming over me, slashing his blade.

There came a bang, the smell of smoke, a large hole developing in Xavier's left shoulder. Blood sprayed from the hole as Xavier collapsed at my feet.

Behind him, struggling to hold the sniper rifle up stood Sam. Even more horrified than Xavier was. His knuckles were white as snow, holding the rifle with an iron grip. Sam was staring at the gun, not quite believing what he just done. Sam had killed someone, pulled the trigger and fired a bullet into another man's back. He had hated how Lewis had killed Sergio, now he had done the same thing. This was going to haunt Sam for The remainder of his life.

"Thanks buddy," I said, clambering out from under the dead weight of Xavier. The dead hand wrapped around my ankle. I shook it off with a shiver and turned to Sam.

Sam still hadn't moved. His eyes were wide and shallow with a fixed gaze on the body.

"I killed him," rasped Sam, shaking on the balls of his feet. He dropped the huge sniper rifle that clattered to the ground with a bang. He still stared at the gun, wary of its power.

"You did kill him," I nodded. "But you saved my life." A thin trail of blood had slid from Xavier's wound, staining the white soles of my shoes.

"Why aren't you terrified," murmured Sam. "How can you not be terrified that some people want to kill us and we killed some of them?" Sam shook on the spot, staring at me intently.

"I've seen so much," I whispered. "They have been many atrocities that W.S.I I'm ashamed to admit I helped orchestrate."

"What stuff," stuttered Sam.

"We can't do this now Sam, we have to go." Something clicked inside Sam and he nodded. He strode forward and opened the door to the garden. "We'll take The Lamborghini." I said but Sam shook his head.

"You crashed the car into the garden," he said. As I entered the garden the carnage I had created shocked me. A towering palm tree had been knocked across the garden and had crashed into the large water feature in the centre of the garden. A huge crack ran up the side of the concrete feature leaking gallons of water across the lawn.

The Lamborghini was crunched into the large rose bushes, a palm tree was stuck in the engine of the car and the windscreen had been shattered.

"This was me?" I gasped, taking in all of the damage I had created.

"You hit the garden at 70mph mate," nodded Sam. "You're lucky you survived with no more than a few bruises."

"But still."

"Better a few trees than you," said Sam, cutting off me completely.

"How do we get away then," I said, as I had dampened our chances of survival. We stood in silence for a few moments until Sam had a bright idea.   "You have other vehicles?" said Sam, smiling to himself, pleased with his *'genius'*

"I don't, I always used my Lamborghini."

"What about your beach buggy."

"What beach buggy?"

"The one in the garage that you took to Menorca," said Sam like I was a dumb six year-old. Without a thank you I dashed across the lawn, weaving through rubble that my crash had created.

I sped at the garage and then stopped the huge door; instinctively I pushed the four digit code into the keypad and lifted the huge door up revealing a cavernous garage. There were fascinating items in the garage but I ignored them all and jumped into the buggy, thankfully the keys were already in it.

I waited for Sam to get in beside me then slamming my foot on the accelerator the beach buggy jolted out of the garage, the vehicle could reach a maximum speed of 40 mph due to illegal modifications Sam had bought.

"Let's go bro," panted Sam but just before I left my driveway a huge almighty sound bellowed from above us.

The sound shook the earth then filled my eardrums. A window on the top floor of my house burst, the glass sparkling and raining down onto the already wrecked garden. Half a second later a fire ball bigger than my car expelled itself from the window and exploded in the air. Small handfuls of fire crashed across the lawn, instantly lighting the garden in a dangerous yellow glow. The boom of the explosion caused me to reactively lift my foot from the accelerator halfway down the round and cup my hands over my ears.

Upstairs thick smoke billowed from the window and distant screams echoed out. Alonzo and Lewis were upstairs amidst the fire.

Flames licked the sky and windowpane, instantly lighting it up in sparks, it was amazing how quickly the fire had spread and was already forming a black fog on the skyline.

"What the-," Sam did not finish his sentence because another huge roar erupted from my house and shook its foundation.

The door burst into orange flames then collapsed, behind it stood a smoky Lewis, unrecognisable due to the ash coating his face. His background was a canvas of yellow, red and orange that had consumed the hall.

It was devastating watching my residence for the past five years collapsing under fire and smoke.

Even from 100 metres away the heat and intensity was almost too much to bare so I had to floor the accelerator. Behind us Lewis dashed towards us at amazing speed reaching the vehicle in 30 seconds. He grabbed the side and hopped onto the back.

"What The hell happened?" I screamed over the crackle of fire and the sound of my house collapsing.

"It wasn't me," choked Lewis in smoke. "Alonzo sparked something in your lab and they came too close to some chemicals."

"So my house was destroyed!"
"And Alonzo," chirped Lewis.

"And my house!"

Shocking Lewis, Alonzo charged out of the charred black skeleton of my house. He looked around for a few seconds then saw us driving away. Alonzo crouched down on one knee, aimed his sub-machine gun and fired. Thankfully

42

his gun was not very accurate so the bullets were not coming within a metre of us. But that was still too close for my liking.

Lewis was giving Alonzo the finger until Sam punched him in the arm.

"Thanks for waiting," said Lewis.

"We didn't wait," I said bluntly. Lewis just sat silently on the back of the buggy.
I could not draw my eyes away from the burning wreck of my house; the west side of the roof had caved inwards, crushing my bedroom and the pool underneath. I could not believe the lab was where the fire had started. When I worked for N.A.S.A I would spend most of my free time in that lab, working on projects. It is there that I had devised the blueprint for the rocket to Mars.

I had been left this in my parents will when I was 10; I had spent the next 7 years desperately waiting to move into it.

I had gone to Westwood, a small foster home for wealthy orphans where I had met Sam. The two of us then moved into this house as soon as possible. It was now burning down to a pile of ash.

I continued off of the drive onto the main road leading to the city centre.

After twenty minutes driving in silence my breathing became easier as there was no sign of us being pursued as we approached the city centre. I felt slightly more normal as we turned onto the high street.

Then a black 4x4 rammed into the side of the buggy and Sam went flying into the road.

The buggy screeched as it rolled down into the high street, full of busy shoppers. The hood of my vehicle crunched, shrapnel flew up, denting the roof. I put my hands over my face in a brace position as I was catapulted forward over the bonnet onto the concrete ground

Pain crackled across my forehead as I felt blood run between my eyes, my vision filled with red as I turned around.

Sam was crawling down the road, his nose replaced with a bloody red mess that was trailing down his chin. A gaggle of shoppers watched his desperate struggle down the road, inch by inch. Alonzo strode up behind Sam and gripped his collar with one of his basketball sized hands.

Sam rose up, flailing and kicking and cursing. Alonzo didn't even flinch as the fists pounded his vast chest.

"Why do you want me?" screamed Sam, choking on the blood running in his mouth.

"I don't want you," snarled Alonzo, shaking Sam like a ragdoll. "I want your scientist friend." Sam opened his mouth to say something but he was suddenly gone. There was a flash of blue and suddenly Lewis was on the other side of the Street, cradling Sam in his arms. Lewis placed Sam on the pavement then leapt across the road at Alonzo. His bare foot collided with Alonzo's chest and sent him flying back into a clothes stand.

Alonzo stood up in the tangle of shirts, fuming at the fact that there might be someone stronger than him. He bounded forward, raging like a rhino, and then punched Lewis square in the jaw. Lewis was sent twirling backwards but managed to catch his balance and landed neatly on the balls on his feet, the blue under his skin fading.

"Get back here you slippery bastard!" roared Alonzo, so angry and red that there might as well be steam coming from his ears.

Lewis pivoted then scooped up Sam, dashing towards me. His hand grabbed my collar and threw me into the driver's seat of Alonzo's open door vehicle.

Lewis was sat next to me and Sam was sat directly behind me, the bleeding had considerably slowed, he held a t-shirt to his face which was caked in dry, black blood.

"Go Joey!" barked Lewis and thankfully Alonzo had left the keys in the ignition; I had no idea where he had got this car though because his car was a burning wreck by my house.

I slammed my feet down on the accelerator, changing gear swiftly.

The huge black vehicle bounced off of the pavement and people dived as I thundered forward, no idea where I was going, just somewhere away from here. The car shot forward still, the market blurring by.

Behind us, his expression a mask of pure fury was Alonzo, he was in a London cab. The cab driver was on the pavement, shaking his fist and swearing at Alonzo.

"We need to go faster!" shouted Sam, leaning out of the window, with his nose bleeding freely on the road as he looked back at Alonzo. His nose was definitely broken but the bleeding had considerably slowed. I realised I was still bleeding from a wound in my forehead, the adrenalin had held the pain back but I knew that soon I would be in pain. My chest and torso were also riddled with purple and black bruises. My knees had been skinned down to the blood that was staining my chinos.

Lewis was covered in more blood, the geyser of blood that had erupted from Sergio was covering his entire left side, the white Manchester United Away shirt he was wearing had been turned red and its value vastly decreased.

"Damn it!" cursed Lewis as Alonzo leant out of his window and fired his weapon. A barrage of bullets hailed against the back windscreen, at first cracks and holes appeared like a large web then the whole thing shattered. Millions of glistening shards showered down as Sam crouched forward. Despite covering his head the glass cut down his neck, huge chunks raking down the back of his head drawing lots of blood. Sam cried out in pain, desperately pulling glass out of his shirt.

"Hang on buddy," I called behind me, spinning the wheel so the car sharply snapped around a corner into an alley, Lewis and Sam were both thrown into the door with a crunch.

Alonzo stopped at the end of the alley and leant out; he grinned and aimed his gun down the alley. Then he squeezed the trigger as a round of bullets shot down the alley and into our car.

The bullets were not close to us fortunately and just created many holes in the ceiling. Sunlight filtered down through the holes, glistening with all of the blood on the seats.

"That was close Sam," I muttered, Lewis was next to me, hanging out of the window. He was watching Alonzo; the distance between us was now too great for Alonzo to shoot us. "Wasn't it Sam," I said, my voice full of worry.

I turned for a second and instantly wished I hadn't. Sam was slumped across the back seats.

A small neat hole had been implanted into his head with a stream of blood running from it. His eyes were dead; he had died instantly after a bullet to the head.

"Sam?" I choked, on the verge of tears. "Sam buddy?" Tears ran down my cheeks and then I turned back to a wall.

Sam watched with dead eyes as the car crunched into concrete and crumpled.

8

The first thing that hit me was the putrid smell, a stink so bad that it made my nose want to shrivel up and die. The vile stench slivered down my throat, wrapping around my oesophagus and choking me. My eyes watered and I gagged at a smell equal to a thousand rotting corpses. It probably was the smell of corpses.

I heard the sounds of bullets around me. But I couldn't see any bullets, or corpses, or anything.

All I could see was complete darkness, so really I couldn't see anything.

I could feel, something squishy underneath me. My hands sunk into a pile of mushy, mud? Sticky syrup interlaced between my fingers.

Painstakingly I dragged my hands out of the muck then edged them forward, in front of my face. My hands pressed against a smooth yet cold surfaced, probably corrugated metal. Why would I be under corrugated metal? I pushed upwards as bangs echoed around me, as I pushed a searing pain shot through my body.

My right arm couldn't push up anymore; it limply fell down to my side and hung there uselessly

After what could have been minutes, or hours, I finally pushed off the iron. It was actually the lid to a green dumpster. I had been lying on top of a pile of rubbish, peelings and cardboard boxes.

I rolled off of the pile into a questionable puddle and lay there for a few minutes until the feeling in my legs returned. That took a while. I stood up and looked around me; I appeared to be in an alley.

Suddenly the memories of today flooded painfully back into me and I was driven to my knees.

Rico trying to kill me, the car chase, Lewis, my house burning down, and Sam. Sam!! What fate had befallen had friend? Was he alive? If so where was he? Where was I?

A splash echoed from behind me. I turned round, not reacting as fast as I should of but still quite fast for me.

Lewis stood in a murky haze, splattered in blood, a black pistol held tightly in his fist. His skin was light blue but as soon as he saw me it faded to its normal colour.

"Are you Ok," muttered Lewis, dropping his gun behind him into the puddle, pretending I didn't notice it.

"You put me in a dumpster," I coughed.

"To protect you."

"Why not behind the dumpster, out of the banana skins?"

"Because it was funny to put you in a dumpster," smiled Lewis, looking like a gleeful child who had done something naughty.

"Where are we? What happened? Sam?"

"Well," huffed Lewis. "Behind a kebab shop, I shot a bunch of dudes and Sam is dead." Despite knowing this already the news still hit me like a lead wrecking ball in the gut. After The deaths of all of the closest people I knew Sam was the only light in the darkness. The only person I had. Now he was dead.

9

Jaden Snow whistled to himself as he walked through the woods, pockets full of cash.

He passed a discarded newspaper on the ground and laughed. On the front cover was a blurry picture of a faceless man in the shadows, the headline read *"Snowman swipes crown jewels."*

Yep, Jaden Snow was no pickpocket, no street urchin. He was master jewel thief 'The Snowman' wanted worldwide. He had stolen The Mona Lisa and hijacked The Oscars, stealing all of the awards.

However he was most proud of his most recent heist, stealing half of the crown jewels, over a trillion pounds worth of jewels in his hands. His sack wasn't big enough to carry the rest.

The crowns, broaches and necklaces were all currently in separate locations Essex, some in his apartment, some buried underground and some even hidden down badger holes.

Overtime Jaden would sell these fine jewels and become rich beyond his wildest dreams. Sexy, charming and rich, that would be the perfect combination, except Jaden already thought of himself as perfect.

As Jaden joyfully hopped through the woods, singing, he thought of his amazing future. However, thanks to the next few minutes, his future couldn't be more different than what he thought it would be like.

Ahead of Jaden stood three men, deep in conversation.

"I have failed," grunted a man with a Spanish accent. Next to the Spanish man a seven foot tall black man stood intimidatingly.

"What!!" snapped the towering man; with a sharp crack the Spanish man was slapped and the force was so great that he was knocked back into a tree.

The third man turned and Jaden instantly recognised him as Rico Angel, his withered old frame was always on the news.

"And you made it public!" screeched Rico, kicking the Spanish man's leg but causing no damage.

"Sorry Uncle," muttered the Spanish man.

"Where are your brothers?" snarled Rico as the Spanish man pulled himself and his pride up.

"Xavier and Sergio have been taken out," answered the Spanish Man. "It wasn't just Tyler and his mate, there was a third dude. I have never seen anyone that skilled with a gun before."

The tall man swivelled round and grabbed Jaden's wrist as he reached into his pocket. Jaden tried to run but the man's grip was too strong.

"Stupid boy!" shouted the man. "What are you doing here? Have you heard anything?"

"I heard nothing," shrugged Jaden, trying to show no fear.

"I will snap your neck!" snarled the man.

"Wait," said Rico coldly, "We need a test subject."

Lewis just stood over pathetic little me, in a puddle. I wasn't crying, just lying. I didn't think I would ever move but eventually I did. I stood up and walked, just walked and walked, closely followed by Lewis. I walked into the street and stood by a battered, rusty, blue mini that had seen better days.

"What's this," I choked, hoping this wasn't our car.

"This is our car," stated Lewis.

"*Our* car?" I asked. "How could you afford this, you have no money."

"I stole from the cash register of a kebab shop," said Lewis with no emotion in his voice. "I also bought us a change of clothes and some McDonalds."

"McDonalds?" I smiled hoping that it would help fill the hole inside me.

After a change of clothes and three cheeseburgers I fell asleep in the front seat as Lewis drove down motorways, I didn't care where he was going, maybe the bottom of the ocean.

My dreams were full of the torturous events of my life; I didn't think things could get worse, so of course they did.

I awoke with a start as the car trundled and rattled up a ramp onto the deck of a boat. The operator of something had his head in my window.

"Oi are you deaf," barked the man. "What's your name?"

"Sam Tyler," I blurted, not even hearing the man's question.

"I'm Lou Tyson," said Lewis.

"Ah, Lou Tyson," yawned the officer. "You're on the list, get in there."

"Lou Tyson?" I said as soon as the officer was out of earshot.

"It's a fake name," said Lewis. "You need one."

10

I woke up, still curled up in the car's front seat, fries and salty packets rolled off of my stomach. My cramped legs needed to stretch so I crawled out of the car into what appeared to be a dark cavern.

It was actually an underground car park with several family cars scattered across the spaces, there wasn't a soul in site, not even Lewis. I was alone in a dark room, a dark swaying cave. Why was the room swaying?

I doubled over and emptied my stomach with a splash, all over the floor. In this vulnerable position I did not notice the man in the black uniform walking across the car park towards me.

"Are you alright mate?" the officer asked. My head turned and I spotted his intimidating Taser, Gun and Pepper spray. The fact that he was wearing W.S.I uniform and had come out of a black W.S.I van made me panic.

I spun around, connecting my fist with the man's jaw; I had the element of surprise so the man was sent off balance and went crashing into an SUV.

"What the -!" cursed the man. He only saw the back of me as I leapt up a set of concrete stairs where the fresh salty air hit me like a brick wall.

I came out onto a rusty deck that had probably been on many voyages over the years. It was crammed with a diversity of people; there were families of squabbling children, young students, old couples, and Lewis!

He was standing by the rails, chatting casually to a Korean couple. They were being sprayed by the unrelenting force of the Ocean and my stomach lurched again. I had always had motion sickness so my parents never took me yachting again after an unfortunate day involving many sick bags.

No regard for manners I tore across the deck and crashed into Lewis.

"W.S.I here," I panted.

"Sorry Jun, sorry Eun," apologised Lewis, "I need to talk with my friend here for a bit."

"It's OK," nodded the woman Tim. "I needed the toilet anyway." She walked off with her husband.

"Where?" urged Lewis as soon as Tim and Eun were out of earshot.

"They'reintheundergroundcarpark, but probably everywhere else on this boat," I said, my words being mangled into a ramble, yet Lewis understood me.

"We have to hide," urged Lewis and then he pulled me towards the lower deck.

Jaden Snow had obviously escaped his cell; he had escaped holding cells, S.W.A.T vans and being trapped in a mansion with thirty policemen, so obviously he had escaped. Alone, he had left the sobbing ginger man and the silent woman; they would just slow him right down. Jaden worked alone. Always leaving his mark.

When Jaden had escaped he did not just leave, he had to rub it in his captors face. Jaden had gone into the captains lounge, emptied the fridge, gone to the toilet without flushing and left a crudely drawn picture on the desk.

Jaden walked out of the captain's lounge in a bathrobe, pockets full of chocolate bars, when two men crashed into him and sent him sprawling to the floor; Jaden saw their faces, faces of people he would bound with on a shattering journey until his demise.

"Are you OK?" I asked.

"What?" spluttered Jaden. "You nearly took my bloody head off."

"But we didn't," shrugged Lewis. "So no harm done then."

"I've got to," blurted Jaden and he scuttled off, down the corridor.

"Wait!" I called. Jaden froze ready to dash. "Is that a Twix in your pocket?" I drooled, noticing the glittering gold wrapper hanging from his pocket.

"Yeah," said Jaden. "Take it." He expertly tossed the bar into my hand and dashed off.

I tore the wrapper off viciously and crammed the bar into my mouth whole. The marvellous flavours swirled around between my cheeks, the chocolate, caramel and shortbread exploding in my mouth. I hadn't eaten a Twix in god knows how long, yet it had always stayed my favourite.

"Who was that?" urged Lewis.

"No one," I said.

"You recognised him. Who is he?" insisted Lewis.

"Jaden Snow. Better known as The Snowman"

"The jewel thief!" gasped Lewis.   .

"How do you know that?" I frowned.

61

"I read a newspaper whilst you were unconscious," said Lewis. "How did you know his real identity?"

"He left so many clues," I answered. "I always wondered why."

"Why don't you ask me," said Jaden.

I swivelled round and Jaden stood with his hands in the air, the man from the car park that I had punched held a compact pistol to his head. Jaden's bathrobe was gone so he was just standing in his underwear. There was a gun in the waistband of Jaden's underwear, the man hadn't noticed.

"Why do you follow us *everywhere*," said Lewis, taunting the man.

"You are wanted dead," snarled the man. "W.S.I will pay good money for your heads."

"It doesn't have to be like this, you don't want to kill anyone," muttered Lewis, edging closer, unbeknown to him.

"Yeah," nodded Jaden. "You don't have to kill the good looking one…. That's me."

"You can't help ," snarled the man. "I need this money for my family."

"We can help," argued Lewis, he took another step forward and the man pulled the trigger. The bang echoed as all hell broke loose.

Lewis acrobatically leapt into the air and landed directly next to him, the bullet was a wild shot and just left a hole in the ceiling. Lewis hit the man with his elbow giving Jaden a chance to bolt towards me.

He shrieked in pain and threw a wild haymaker which Lewis ducked under. Lewis then delivered two expertly delivered punches into his gut that tore his stomach muscles.

BANG!!!

Lewis had pulled the guns trigger against the back of the man's neck.

The man tripped to the ground, a pool of blood spreading around a hole in his neck. You could clearly see through his severely damaged windpipe.

Another W.S.I man ran forward, beating his fists onto Lewis' face and chest. These expertly delivered blows were powerful but Lewis didn't feel from something like this. He just stood as the W.S.I man punched him with all of his training as Lewis' blue glow of his skin faded and his killing streak dispersed.

With his punches providing minimal effect the enemy drew a gun and aimed at Lewis. Lewis just flicked his wrist into the man's chest and he cracked against the wall. He lay there moaning as the man, named Tim, thought that maybe he death would be better now because he had missed a chance to kill the target.

"Why'd you do that?" asked Jaden.

Lewis had no answer; he had been faced with a danger so he had removed the danger.

"Well," said Jaden. "Thanks for saving me, I have to go."

"No," I blurted, grabbing Jaden's arm. "You're with us Snowman."

Jaden spun and grabbed my neck. "How do you know that," snarled Jaden.

My mouth opened and I started speaking when an eruption behind us shut us up and sent us flying into the wall. My limp arm cracked against plasterboard sending flurries of pain up my nervous system.

Alonzo and five goons thundered down the corridor, guns blazing. A bullet clipped Lewis' arm but he had already reached his blue killing spree so didn't notice.

The unfortunate man who had fired the bullet was grabbed round the throat by a blue hand and tossed into the air.

Lewis took the man's fallen gun and shot him before he hit the floor. He then ran down the side of the corridor and gracefully sprung into the air, his hands reached a man's waist. He took the man's knife and jammed it into flesh. Two goons down, four to go.

Lewis pivoted and brought the knife down onto Alonzo, who expertly sidestepped so the bullet raked down Alonzo's ear, taking the whole thing off.

Blood exploded into the air and sprayed over the three remaining men. The scarlet fountain obscuring their vision as Alonzo writhed on the ground, and no one stepped in to aid him.

Me and Jaden lay on the ground, Jaden gripped a pistol but did nothing with, just lay there.

Lewis advanced towards the remaining men, hatred boiling over inside him, when his whole body shuddered, volts surged through him and he collapsed, his muscles having erratic spasms on the ground.

Behind him stood a shaky adolescent who couldn't have been older than 19 years old, a glowing blue Taser gripped in his palms, a wire extended from The Taser to Lewis's spine.

"Finally someone doing something right," grunted Alonzo, blood pouring over his face and chest.

Two men hurried over to Alonzo with bandages and med kits, tending to his ear.

"And someone sort out those two bastards," roared Alonzo, waggling his bloody finger at me and Jaden.

I shoved Jaden up and bolted down the corridor with new energy that I thought would never return to me. My legs worked mechanically trying to get away, heavily pursued my four armed men.

Jaden rolled across the bloody carpet and raised his gun to a man's face. A bullet created a neat, red hole in the centre of the man's face.

He would have been able to let off a few more shots if a huge baton hadn't of whacked him in his temple. There was a comical clang as Jaden slipped from consciousness and his eyes rolled back in his head.

Jaden dreamed the money he may eventually make if he sold the crown jewels as he gently snoozed.

Meanwhile I was pinned to the floor by two men; they were fixing heavy iron handcuffs to my wrists and pointing and hot pistols to the back of my neck. It singed all of the hairs down my neck and would probably leave a burn mark.

I wriggled but the flat palm on my between my shoulder blades was restricting all of my movement. I could shift my arms to make a grab at for the gun.

"Let go of me," I grumbled into the shag carpet, thrashing my limbs at the floor.

"Shut the hell up or I may have to put a bullet in your brain," snapped the man with the gun to my head. He made sure to do up my handcuffs extra tight so they were digging into my wrists as I was humiliatingly frog marched to Alonzo.

Alonzo was sitting on a fold-up chair, his head wrapped in black stained bandages that leaked red over Alonzo's left shoulder.

"Rico wants you," said Alonzo in a flat dark voice. "He will. Ah! Son of a b-." One of Alonzo's medics had dug in a bit too much and received a huge fist to the gut for causing Alonzo pain.

"Take him away!" shrieked Alonzo, his red finger pointing to my left. The pain was obviously obscuring Alonzo's mind.

"Hold on!" I objected but the barrel of a gun smashed into my skull before I could intervene further. I fell to my knees and then flat onto my face as a thin trickle of liquid slipped down the back of my neck.

My vision failed me, darkness flooding all of my senses, emptying my mind.

Alonzo stood up and pushed one the men tending to his wounds into a wall. He strode over to Tim and held a blood-soaked pistol to Tim's snivelling, tear-streaked face.

"Give me a good reason why I shouldn't blow your face off in ten seconds! You let the boys escape. The other one who did that is already dead so that only leaves you!" roared Alonzo, spittle flying into Tim's bleary eyes.

Tim looked up and opened his mouth but only a muffled squeak came out.

"10....9....8!"

"Wait!" cried Tim. "I can help you."

"How could you possibly help?" snarled Alonzo. He was not expecting an answer but what Tim did was even more surprising. Tim kicked Alonzo straight between the legs then was gone.

The men went to chase him round the corner but Alonzo stopped them with a big, beefy bicep.

"This one is mine," Alonzo groaned. He checked the clip on his pistol, straightened his trousers then strode around the corner.

Tim collided with a door and desperately banged his fists against it.

"Please!" plead Tim. "Open up!" Alonzo marched down towards Tim, levelling his gun at her head, his thick fingers by the trigger.

"No one will get away with kicking me," barked Alonzo, a thick, blue vein bulging on his neck.

"B-." A bullet tore through Tim's shoulder blade, splintering all of the cartilage; stark white bone tore through Tim's shoulder, tearing a huge gash down his neck. In seconds the sleeves on Tim's shirt were soaked in crimson liquid that trailed over the carpet.

Tim closed her eyes and whimpered, and then he fell silent.

11

Kane Cliffton strode through the long winding corridor, sweat rolling down his forehead. He was flanked by two burly guards with muscles bulging through their shirts that were imprinted, in big yellow block letters, with the letters W.S.I.

Finally Kane was guided to a black door labelled *Mr R.Angel,* Kane stood anxiously as the door was pushed open by one of the guards. Kane couldn't help noticing the huge glocks hanging from their belts.

"Come in Mr Cliffton," grinned Rico Angel, a sinister tone in his voice.

"Thank you, sir," mumbled Kane, keeping his eyes fixed on the ground.

"Please," muttered Rico. "Take a seat." Kane sat down in the seat in front of Rico.

"Tell me about yourself then, Kane," said Rico with a smile of well-maintained teeth with a yellow tint due to his heavy smoking of cigars. Kane spotted specks of blood on Rico's cuffs, fresh blood.

"I'm an orphan so I was raised in an orphanage since I was a baby. I don't know anything about my origins but through DNA tests they have discovered Jamaican and Irish roots in my blood," said Kane, stuttering a bit with anxiety.

"Interesting," nodded Rico. "Why do you want to work here?"

"I've had a history of violence," sighed Kane, slightly ashamed. "I am a black belt in Karate and figured if I'm going to get a job it should be something where I can use my skills."

"You're hired," said Rico abruptly.

"What?" Kane spluttered. "Aren't you going to ask me any more questions?"

"That isn't needed. We recently been short staffed due to a predicament and could use as much help as possible."
"

"Thank you," said Kane, he stood up and left the room.

"Bye Mr Cliffton."

Kane left smiling, one step closer to discovering the truth. This position would surely help him uncover the reasons of his father's disappearance years ago.

Rico watched the boy leave then yanked his draw open. On top of tedious paperwork and files was a cylindrical cardboard box that had seen better days. Anxiously Rico tears the lid off of the box and reveals two brown, leaf-wrapped cigars and a lighter, exactly where they should be. Rico drew out one of the expensive cigars and clamps it between his yellow teeth. He then picks up the lighter and flicks the cap, lighting up the cigar.

"Good," smiled Rico through a puff of pungent smoke. Rico was a heavy smoker and had found that these exotic Cuban cigars calmed his nerves and relaxed him. Clouds of brown smoke drifted across the ceiling and were pulled out of the window by a sudden gust of wind.

Rico had lured in another man to his company, with what was coming he would need as many expendable men as possible.

Cigars truly were the only way to keep cool, them and whiskey.

Sitting at an angle, resting under Rico's thigh was a black leather suitcase; it was locked with seven combinations, retina scan, finger print, voice activation and was bullet proof. The contents were almost as precious to Rico as his life, almost.

The papers inside Rico had read over a hundred times, basking in joy.

To find the Monster that you seek,

Travel to a known antique,
Through a thriving yet dead land,
Dominated by time and sand,
To bring the beast from the his constricting
pool,
Take the soul of someone cruel,
If you don't wish to be the beasts eat,
Find the soul of someone sweet,
Finally you'll need the key,
Locked away for eternity,
Until you kill its second part,
Just be warned he is smart,

Rico thought he knew who the key was, and he was currently in one of his holding cells with the boy who had discovered the documents.

Rico chuckled.

I think I'd been awake a long time, just staring at the ceiling; maybe, I could just see darkness, shadows, black. Someone could be half an inch in front of me, waving their guns, claws and knives in my face and I would have no clue. All my other senses worked, my hands were feeling a smooth metal surface, and it was cold, too cold. A shiver went up my spine.

I could hear a whimpering in the corner, a light sobbing, it was full of pain. That wasn't the only sound, there was breathing behind me natural breathes every few seconds. They may be staring at me planning an attack.

My mother had said to me that if you can't see the monsters then they can't see you. I said that wasn't true but right now I hoped that more than anything.

"Hello!" My head snapped round as fast as humanly possible and I stood up. A jolt of pain shot up my arm like a firework and I clutched it.

"Hello," came the voice again. "What's happening?" The voice was soft and almost a whimper but I recognised it, definitely.

"Who are you?" I called out, trying to define where the voice was coming from. My head was pounding now and my arm felt like it was on fire but I tried to sound natural.

"Ollie Tripton," snivelled the voice, I was certain I knew the voice. "Where am I?"

"I wish I knew," I muttered grimly, and then I fell to my knees.

"Are you Ok man?" said Ollie.

I looked up and saw nothing. "How can you see me?" I said, anxiety filling my voice.

"With my eyes." The truth hit me like a ten tonne boulder, it smashed me down and as I tried to get back up it flattened me again, I was blind! The knock to my head could have dislodged something or damaged my brain but all I knew was that I couldn't see.

I screamed out then sobbed, I couldn't see but I could still sense Ollie watching me, wandering what to do.

"What's going on?" said a new voice. Me and Ollie were not alone. "Ollie, where are we?" This voice was female, I was certain; it was a soft, kind voice that flowed like caramel.

"I think Joey can't see anything," said Ollie to the girl. I wondered how this stranger knew my name. I opened my mouth but it was like Ollie had read my mind.

"You're Joey Tyler world famous billionaire," stated Ollie. "Of course I recognise you, even though the newspapers say you are dead.

"What!?" I snapped. "How?"

"I read that," said the feminine voice. "You died when some chemicals caught fire and your house burned down. Millions of pounds worth of antiques destroyed in one."

Could my life get worse?

"What do we do now?" I pleaded, my heart had deflated and I had nothing else left. My house destroyed, best friend murdered and now my vision was gone.

Ollie and the girl just sat in silence, it could have been minutes or hours but they just sat opposite or behind me, watching.

BANG!!

A huge noise echoed around, the sheer volume of the crash made my ears ring and my teeth chatter. There was another bang from the force of an impact then a horrible scraping noise that made my hair stand up on ends. A whoosh of air blew over my head and then there was an explosion of noise behind me.

"Hello people, your saviour has arrived. Please, adore me later," The voice lit my heart with joy. Lewis!

"Let's go Joey boy, me main man," giggled Lewis. "Get over here."

"I have a slight problem," I whispered nervously. "I can't see."

Lewis must have been just as shell shocked as me because he stood in silence for a few seconds without speaking until another set of footsteps rapidly approached.

"Hurry up guys," shouted Jaden over sudden gun fire, and then he ran off.

"What now," I muttered, shamefully looking at the ground, or where I thought the ground should be.

I felt something grab my arm and pull me onto a chunk of something muscly, my hands gripped onto the bumps of Lewis' shoulders.

"Hold on." Then I was shooting down a corridor, the wind whipping around me. I heard explosions and gunfire, shouts and screams. The air smelt like a heavy mist of blood. I had no idea what was happening but it sounded like a war was taking place.

A huge fiery explosion rattled my skull and I felt my body crash against what could have been the soft squishy flesh of a body.

Water seeped around me, dampening my clothes and soul. I gasped and felt the cold sea sliver down my throat.

I tried to stand up but my body, refused to do anything. All I could do was lay as the unrelenting fury of the Ocean rose above my face. Bile rose in my throat and into the water.

Jaden waded through waist-deep water to an exit; to his left were Ollie and his right, Angelique. That was the mystery girls name; it was a French name meaning angel, Angelique.

A hole as big as a head was gushing in gallons of seawater and sinking the ship like it was made of lead. After Lewis had busted out of his cell there had been a fire fight and someone had a grenade, the effect of the explosion tore a gaping hole in the ship. Jaden, Ollie and Angelique were desperately trying to escape an underwater tomb; whilst they had been fighting their way out all of the civilians had escaped on lifeboats leaving only a few.

A man swam around the corner and as soon as Jaden spotted his W.S.I uniform he shot him in the head.

"Why did you do that!" snapped Ollie, obviously not liking violence.

"He was an enemy. I shot him in the head," shrugged Jaden and he waded off followed by Ollie and Angelique trying to catch up. The water was now about chest height and was rising increasingly faster; soon they would be fully submerged.

Suddenly, from under the water, a W.S.I burst out, gasping for breath. His eyes grew wide when he saw Jaden and the gun. Jaden made a lunge chop with his pistol but the man disarmed him and held the pistol to Jaden's temple.

Ollie and Angelique stood transfixed, as Jaden prepared to be shot.

Lewis barrelled down the corridor, as I clutched desperately to his back. I was dropped into the water with a loud splash as Lewis leapt forward onto the man. As I flailed under the waves finally returning to the surface there was the sound of a sort struggle then a sickening crunch that made Ollie gag.

"Thanks mate," said Jaden, sounding ashamed because he had been overpowered.

"Now what," I said, apparently facing the wall, my clothes drenched.

Lewis' hand grabbed my forearm and it glowed so blue I could actually see its turquoise outline, the blue shone into me and I felt the light spread across my body, creating a tingling. Then it burned, a pain like hot lava was slivering up my arm and across my body. My arms suddenly felt like lead and I slipped under the water. Spasms ripped across my body, my limbs writhed and I opened my mouth to scream but I couldn't.

My eyelids flipped open to the scene of the ongoing battle and I felt renewed, I had been recharged and it felt great. Then I saw her, a perfectly chiselled face with smooth blonde hair perfectly placed on her head. She looked so delicate like a gust of wind could tear her in two.

"Are you Ok?" asked Angelique in her light French accent.

"Yeah," I slurred and pulled myself up. My head hit the ceiling and I went back down.

I was in a, a, broom cupboard. It was a cramped dark square with glistening cobwebs in the corner. Outside was gunfire, I had to know what was happening.

So I barged out onto the top deck of the boat. Alonzo, still bloodied and battered, was screaming orders at his men who were firing machine guns across the deck at Lewis who leapt from side to side, firing his pistol. There were only ten men firing at Lewis and I think that's how Alonzo had left.

Jaden was behind Lewis and he pushed Ollie into a lifeboat that, then he gestured to me and Angelique. We sprinted across the battlefield as Lewis covered us with his expert shots. I ran past Lewis as he fired a bullet into a man's skull then shot another man in the gut.

Angelique and I dived over the edge of the boat onto the rubber lifeboat. I noticed that the water was barely up the top deck of the boat. We can't have been in very deep waters because the boat had sunk and reached the bottom of this stretch of water.

"Hold on," shouted Jaden, he shot the rope holding us in place, then kicked the life boat. Huge waves dragged us away from the battle and sea spray battered us until we had no sense of direction.

The life raft was yanked this way and that way until the distant boat looked minuscule. Small black lump, miles away. It shook slightly then a pillar of huge orange flames rose high into the sky and spread out like a giant fiery muffin.

The black smoke billowed out across the sky and spread into the clouds, turning the sky into black smog. Then the bang came, the noise echoed across the water and sent waves of water high into the sky. Our boat was thrown back a few dozen metres and it flipped over, we were engulfed in freezing channel water. The salty brine washed over me and froze me to my bones. Seawater seeped into all of my crevices and into my mouth. The taste was bitter and made me gag, I would have vomited but my stomach was empty. Plus my throat was full of the sea.

I shivered under the waves then felt uncomfortably cold hands grab my shoulders and dragged me up onto the boat.

"Help," croaked Ollie as he was yanked under the surface again. I extended my arm which Ollie gratefully grabbed and pulled himself onto the boat. We lay there, sprawled out until Jaden poked me with his foot.

"Get up Joey, it's just freezing cold water."

"What are you doing?" I snapped. "What happened?"

Small flecks of ash rained from the sky like snowflakes and plastered our clothes; a large piece of shrapnel fell down a foot from my head and created an almighty splash that made me jump up. A chunk of metal had been launched sky high off of the boat. The ferry had been completely demolished by explosions and now lay on the shallow seabed. Yet Alonzo survived, his remaining men escaped in another lifeboat in the other directions. "The boat went boom," said Angelique, struggling with English which was not her first language.

"Lewis blew those bastards down to the ocean floor," nodded Jaden.

Lewis was dead then. I figured there was no way he could have survived the explosion and the boat sinking. I didn't feel any emotion at that point.

From behind came a familiar voice as a head bobbed from the waves "Yep, I blew them up," yawned Lewis as he pulled himself from the sea onto the boat.

Rico loved the way the plan looked, melded metal titanium grafted with a beating heart and an energy cannon, the pinnacle of human strength in one man. He would have unmatched strength. Now Rico just needed a body.

Kane put the phone down after hanging up, after a long conversation with his long-term friend Will he had decided he would head to The W.S.I base in central Europe, he was unsure of the bases exact location but that was where he would ask to be transferred. As far as he knew that's where is cousin was going to be detained. At least he hoped it was his cousin. It was here that Kane and two other people he had teamed up with would find Joey and if necessary help him escape. After hours of extensive research through the W.S.I records of all employees and families he had deduced that somehow Joey Tyler was his cousin. His father had been killed in the same accidental explosion that had killed his father. Well the public thought the explosion was an accident.

He had so many questions to ask and hoped his cousin would be in a condition to answer dozens.

Conor Oak sat alone on his bed, his only friend a bottle of *Bourbon*. W.S.I were animals, cruel soulless monsters intent on getting their way. They had committed unspeakable atrocities to Conor and now wanted him to commit one himself.

Conor's best friend Jaden had just landed in France and W.S.I wanted Conor to bring him in. Conor had attempted to fight back, thinking his five years in Afghanistan special ops would help him but they had found his only weak spot and now they were using him like a pawn.

Poor Jaden wouldn't see it coming and he would be taken. But it is for the better good, Conor convinced himself. He took a long deep sip from the bottle and collapsed.

At the moment I was in no condition to do anything, my legs are arms were black with bruises and my head pounded. I lay on a Calais beach as the Sea lapped around my ankles and the sand flowed into my clothes. The breeze whistled past my ear, whispering silent messages.

Back on the boat Lewis had done the most amazing thing; he had started shining blue, grabbed the back of our lifeboat and pushèd us. We hurtled across the tides at amazing speeds and within ten minutes we had hit the beach. The four of us were flung into the air like ragdolls and landed on the sand.

We now lay here. Taking in the peace and quiet, it was only the early hours of the morning so the normally busy town was deserted, a few rowdy drunks sang from the town square and a couple lay togeTher further down the beach.

So apart from that we lay alone, eventually it was Jaden who broke the spell of silent serenity.

"So, where to know Papa Smurf?" said Jaden as he stared at Lewis' skin which had only just died down to its natural colour. Lewis didn't realise this was an insult and answered.

"We need to lay low, find a motel and stay in there a few days," said Lewis.

"I have a friend who lives around here, we could stay at his," suggested Jaden.

"But W.S.I probably know that and are keeping tabs on him," intervened Ollie.

"No I haven't seen him in years, last I saw him was a while back."

I wasn't really paying attention to the conversation I was looking at Angelique to my left in the sand dune, her golden hair spread across the soft beach. Her eyes were only half open; she was slowly drifting into sleep whilst trying to focus on the conversation.

"Joey! Joey I asked you what you think," yelled Lewis in my ear.

"What?!" I spluttered, taking in a mouthful of sand and salty water. "I like Lewis' idea of a motel."

"What if we're attacked?" asked Angelique, her question swallowed by a yawn.

"Jaden has a gun," stated Lewis, Then he trudged off onto the road directly adjacent to the beach that lead into town.

I was soaking wet, freezing and I exhausted but I stood up and reluctantly followed Lewis, closely trailed by the rest.

We tramped down cobbled roads and past small stalls preparing for the morning market until we came to what looked like a glowing holiday inn. The sign was in French but even my limited French vocab could make out that it contained The word '*hôtel*' It was tall, about 15 floors, and was lined with rows of balconies that had a view of the whole of Calais. The lights were out in nearly all of the rooms except for a sole few.

"We should go in here," said Lewis and everyone else mumbled in agreement as we were too tired to argue.

A blast of friendly warm air hit us as we passed through a set of automatic doors into a plush, cavernous reception. An exhausted receptionist sat behind a long desk with a fake smile plastered on her face and turned it towards us as we entered. She seemed the least bit surprised at five dripping wet people who looked like they had been in a warzone, mainly because we had been in a warzone.

A square table that needed a clean was covered with dusty board games that hadn't been touched in years. It was surrounded by torn white sofas that had a peculiar stain across the arm.

The only appealing part of this area was the delicious smell wafting from the restaurant to my left. The smell of bacon, sausages and hash browns drifted into my nostrils and made my stomach growl.

I read a sign that I think said the restaurant would not open until 6:00am, half an hour away! I was ravenous and didn't think I could wait half an hour until eating.

"I've got this," grinned Jaden. He strode up to the desk with a smug smile implanted on his face and leant on the counter getting seawater in the desk but the receptionist didn't seem to care.

"Trois chambres, veuillez," smiled Jaden, leaning closer to the woman.

"D'accord," giggled the receptionist.

A few more French words were spoken Then Jaden produced a few crisp Euro notes and placed them in the receptionists hand after being handed three keys numbered 216-218.

"Merci," smirked Jaden as he sidled away towards us then placed the keys in my palm.

"Where did you get that money?" I asked.

"That loving couple on the beach seemed not to notice their money being taken," said Jaden.

"You stole it," gasped Ollie.

"For the greater good," shrugged Jaden and then he marched the elevator and pressed the button for the 5th floor.

The silver, scratched doors dinged open and we all filed inside just as they shut with a clang. It was cramped in the small metal box as it rose and we all smelled like seafood so I was grateful when the elevator came to a stop and we all clambered over each other onto the red shag carpet.

The corridor was completely unfurnished with plain white walls that were with dozens of plain oak doors.

Out of our three adjoining rooms Angelique got the left one to herself, Ollie and Jaden had to share the middle room (which Ollie wasn't particularly happy about) and me and Lewis shared the final room. All of the rooms were connected by doors so we were all together.

91

"Do I have to go with him," moaned Ollie like an annoyed five year old. "He'll steal my wallet."

"You don't have a wallet on you," pointed out Jaden.

"Well if I did you would steal it," said Ollie and he marched into his room.

My room was plain, that was the only word to describe it. Two single beds in a white-washed room, opposite a huge mirror next to an unmarked door.

"I'm showering first!" I shouted and charged through the door into a miniscule bathroom. I dropped my clothes and jumped into the shower/bath, instantly I shivered as a jet of freezing water washed over me. I yelped and leapt high into the air but eventually the water heated up.

It felt great, the tepid water pouring over my skin, warming me up inside and out. The water plastered my hair to my scalp; I was completely serene until I noticed the trail of blood being sucked down the drain! Dried blood was being washed off of dozens of tiny cuts. My arms were bombarded with ugly black and blue bruises and dirt had encrusted itself deep under my fingernails so it looked like I would never be fully clean.

I stayed in the shower for a very long time and at long last when I got out it was because of my hunger. I left my clothes and put on a bathrobe that was hung on the back of the bathroom door.

I glided into my room following my nose down a few flights of stairs into the reception and then around noisy families into the restaurant.

Jaden, Ollie and Angelique sat around a table with plates piled high with delicious smelling food; however I did not notice them because my eyes were drawn towards the huge buffet. Eggs, bacon, grits, sausage. All piled up waiting for me. To the left there was even a table of cakes and doughnuts.

I charged across the restaurant, picked up a plate and started piling as much food as I could fit onto one plate then poured maple syrup over the Mountain of meat and pancakes.

"Hi," smiled Angelique as I sat down. However I could not answer because my mouth was already crammed full with bacon.

"Where's Lewis?" asked Ollie. I just shrugged and jammed a pancake between my jaws.

After I had wolfed down my food in ten minutes Jaden asked me a question. "My mate who lives around here is coming down here later; he said he may know a way out of the country."

"I still think it's a bad idea," grumbled Ollie. "He is probably being tracked."

"Well he is already on his way with some big guns and cash," snapped Jaden. "So you can't do anything about it, squirt."

"Why do you need cash, you seem fine stealing the money off of that couple," scorned Ollie, acid in his voice.

"I stepped up when no one else did and saved the day," he shot back. Ollie did not answer and just ate his bacon leaving Jaden feeling like the winner.

"It's not a good idea but we can't do anything else so we have to wait for him to get here," I said after swallowing my last scrap of waffles.

"Where's Lewis," asked Angelique trying to ease the tension.

"I don't know I admitted. He wasn't in the room when I got out of the shower."

"Probably in trouble," scoffed Jaden before standing up and heading to the buffet for some sausages.

"He'll probably turn up," I said, and he did. Lewis and another man came flying over the banisters off the stairs onto my breakfast!

Cal Adrians, codename One, stood in the busy town centre, a suburban trading market in Brazil. The wool satchel was slung over his shoulder, weighed down by the blue bladed dagger that had a complicated foreign name which One had no chance of pronouncing correctly.

One had risked his life in an underground cavern for this staff and he was not going to lose it, Mr Drake had been very eager for him to retrieve this staff, he says it would destroy the immortal. One said that if you were immortal you couldn't be killed and that gained him a powerful blow to the face.

Well what did one know he was a freak, which is what everyone else had called him 'freak'.

One rarely spoke, kids would approach him, try to bully him Then he would say what they were thinking and embarrass them; that was all he ever did. But then he discovered that he was a great fighter, a boy tried to pick on one, started pushing him The One hit the boy and knocked him unconscious, he was 8. Then no one would ever fight him, or speak to him, they were too scared.

One had a lot of free time so with the tiny allowance his orphanage gave him he bought French textbooks, then Spanish, German and Chinese.

Now One spoke 13 different languages and was an expert in dozens of fighting styles, The perfect assassin. Dillon Drake had snatched One up and hired him straight away.

His Pay-as-You-Go phone beeped and he opened a picture with The caption 'Kill', he left to kill Joey Tyler.

12

"Why were you in my room?" screamed Lewis, his hand around a neck as thick as a tree trunk.

"I was.. I was looki…" The man choked, maple syrup was splattered up the side of his head, making his hair messy and sticky. The man hefted his arms forward and shoved Lewis back with the strength of ten men. However Lewis was still stronger and pulled the man back with him bringing them into The carpet among plates of bacon.

The man swung a wild haymaker aiming for Lewis' head but Jaden grabbed his arm a split second before contact.

"Conor don't," shouted Jaden. "He's on our team."

"What?" spluttered the man apparently named Conor. "This lunatic attacked me."

"You was in my room!" Lewis screamed in Conor's face, spittle flying all over him. "Looking through my stuff."

"I just went to the room Jaden told me to go to that room and I wanted to be certain it was his room," growled Conor.

"We'll have you heard of knocking," snarled Lewis but his ferocity was fading and his skin was reverting to its normal colour.

"Have you heard of anger management," Conor snapped back. Lewis had no reply so he increased his grip on Conor's throat then let go and walked away. Conor sat up and rubbed the purple marks on his throat.

"Ignore him," said Jaden helping Conor up, "Lewis can be a bit of trouble but he saved my life and now, unfortunately, I owe him. Anyway I already looked through his stuff, there was nothing there."

Conor grunted and walked towards the stairs up to our room, he could ignore the dozens of pairs of eyes staring at us and the wreck we had caused. However I could feel every eye burning into the back of my head.

"What's this then?" asked Lewis, he had picked up a small photo off of the ground that had fallen out of Conor's pocket.

I looked curiously over Lewis' shoulder and saw a picture of Conor with his tree trunk arm around a beautiful woman with a baby that couldn't be older than a week in his arms.

"That's mine," grunted Conor, he yanked the photo from Lewis' fingers and stormed off.

"That's his wife and kid," muttered Jaden, his jovial tone vanishing into the air. "They went missing."

Kane Cliffton walked down the French high street towards the sound of screaming and where the stench of smoke intensifies, small flecks of ash fluttered down from the clouds and landed on Kane's mop of black hair, singing it slightly.

Ahead a red glow licked the skyline and radiated heat that could be felt from a quarter of a mile away.

A blackened man jogged by but stopped to speak to Kane.

"Where are you going man, the whole block up there is up in flames, it is all sectioned off," panted the man. "Keep away unless you want to go up in flames."

Before Kane could utter a thank you the man ran off away from the fire. Kane, however, continued towards the fire it was possibly the only way he could discover the truth. Joey Tyler had been spotted here 30 minutes ago and he could still be here. This could be the moment where Kane was united with a family member. The moment when we wasn't almost completely alone in the world. Well it would have been if The *Holiday Inn* hadn't burned down 10 minutes ago.

Kane only came across a police tape and fire fighters trying to battle a fire that had consumed the whole building.

1 hour earlier

Dillon Drake had been lead here by his master, his lord, older than time itself and as wiser than any man ever will be. That wisdom was now trapped physically, had been that way for over 1000 years but mentally he was with Dillon, could speak to him and command him and Dillon would always obey, he had just kidnapped Rico Angel and put him on an unmarked train. All for the cause. He could not fail because his master would never forgive him, Dillon had failed his master once and he had paid dearly for it. He felt his left eye, well what remained of it, the entire eye was gone leaving a blank socket a reminder that he was indebted to his master forever and could never fail. His master had tried to return to our Earth and been defeated by the only other like him, it had been Dillon's job to kill the hindrance to the plans, anyone who had helped the boy that had messes up his masters plans were killed, the boy disappeared. Soon his

unknown master '*The Ignotus*' would return to
this world and wreck this world, destroy whole
continents and take the lives of every worthless
human being on this planet. But for his saviour
to return Dillon must first destroy a human,
nothing more than an irritating itch on his plan a
pimple to be popped but it had to be done. Soon
Joey Tyler would be eliminated and everything
would fall into place.

Dillon walked into the lobby but he did not
anticipate what would happen, the blonde haired
boy whose skin glowed a slight faded turquoise.
Dillon walked towards Joey; his target was sat at
a table with a girl and a ginger boy, the blonde
boy stood a few feet away.

Dillon picked up pace, jogging across The
plaza, now sprinting straight at Joey, he was
close so close. His fist swung in an arching
motion with a force that would have knocked
Joey's head clean off. Would have if it wasn't
for the blonde boy.

Dillon's armed moved as a blur, so fast that
Joey couldn't react, but Lewis did, he shot across
the room and grabbed Dillon's arm twisting it in

a way that would break any normal man's arm. Dillon was not a normal man.

Lewis' eyes widened in shock as Dillon threw a tremendous earthquake of a punch into his face, Lewis' head snapped back and he flew 40 feet through several walls.

"What the hell!" I shouted as I watched Lewis fly backwards meaning that The incredibly strong man's attention was turned straight towards me, all of his strength thrown into a single punch flew at my neck but before contact Lewis came hurtling across the tables and collided with the man (whose name I would later discover to be Dillon) knocking them into the stairs which shattered under the force. Now people were running and screaming; fearing for their lives.

I threw myself to the floor then scrambled for the exit no idea what was going on, I crawled forward closely followed by Ollie and Angelique. I had no idea where Conor and Jaden were I had last seen them go upstairs.

"What's happening!" screamed Angelique over the sound of screaming people.

"I… !" Lewis shot by me and hit a table, reducing it to splinters. Dillon walked calmly towards him, talking to an earpiece he had on.

"This is Team Alpha-17 requesting backup from team Tango-65 location mission place number 1452," said Dillon, still advancing towards me. I fell backwards and tried to crawl under the table but Dillon grabbed my ankle and yanked me up, holding me in the air.

"I have been instructed to terminate you, or at least get you out of the way," growled Dillon. "Two of your friends however I have instructed to keep alive but I can have all of the fun I want with him."

"Why don't you just kill me then?" I choked, all of the blood rushing to my head.

"That is what I will do them," smiled Dillon and he flipped me over in an impossible manoeuvre that left him holding me by my throat, crushing my larynx. I felt my last breathe escape me and my vision fading but before I reached my final destination Dillon dropped me onto the floor and turned around, I could see dozens of tiny red holes in his back that were closing up.

Conor and Jaden were upstairs firing short bursts from machine guns at Dillon. They were both fantastic shots and every single bullet hit Dillon, some ricocheted off of his skin and flew in random directions whilst others found weak spots and penetrated his skin. Unfortunately these only created small pocket holes that soon closed up leaving no real damage to Dillon.

Thanks to Jaden's and Conor's distraction I was able to run away and dive underneath one of the few remaining tables. Dillon turned towards me but found Ollie cowering by a chair.

"What do you want," snivelled Ollie as a hand reached for his throat.

"I have no need for you, earth scum," snarled Dillon. "I need her." His finger was aimed at Angelique who was running away. Dillon crouched and then leapt up in one motion that resulted with him landing directly in front of her. Angelique's eyes lit up with fear and her mouth opened as Dillon's hand snatched her by the neck and turned on his heels.

Ollie charged forward but Dillon swung a haymaker that threw him back into the receptionist's counter, his head smacked against the desk knocking him instantly unconscious. He slumped to the floor and a thin trail of blood seeped from his hairline.

Jaden and Conor had to stop firing for fear of hitting Angelique and because the stairs had been obliterated they were stranded upstairs, the only way down was a 10 foot drop.

Lewis shot out like a rocket, glowing a shade of blue that hurt my eyes it was so bright, for a split second I saw Lewis' face, an expression of snarling fury and pure hatred that would consume any man.

Lewis, the bolt of blue lightning, struck Dillon. The palm of Dillon's hand and was held in the air. He was held four feet off of the floor Dillon's beefy hand crushing his collarbone and causing stark white bones to splinter out from under his skin. Dillon increased the force of his squeeze and Lewis started to lose consciousness, his vision went black and when he finally slipped into a deep sleep Dillon casually tossed him into the kitchen. Lewis' heavy body reduced the kitchen door to kindling.

Dillon marched out carrying the screaming Angelique; she kicked and struggled but was no match for Dillon's brute strength.

"Stop struggling!" growled Dillon. "You will be restrained." Dillon's voice did not sound like his own it was layered like several people were talking at the same time and there was a deeper resonation like the voice of an old man, gravelly and not focused.

"Never!" screeched Angelique, her voice going hoarse and scratchy, she continually kicked at Dillon but it was not having the desired effect, Dillon just flicked a wrist in her direction and his finger caught the bridge of her nose, Angelique's body went rigid and her back arched over Dillon's shoulder.

I lay under the table waiting for someone to spring into action and save Angelique but I realised that there was no one left to save Angelique, Ollie and Lewis were unconscious whilst Conor and Jaden were still stuck at the top of the stairs.

That left only me to do something quickly, and I did, I picked up a smashed plate with a syrup stain and threw it across the debris of the restaurant, the china disc struck the back of Dillon's neck and shattered doing little more than irritate him. Dillon swiped at the air then turned on me.

"Put her down!" I squeaked, that was supposed to sound masculine and brave but I got caught on my words and it sounded like a hamster.

"You dare defy me, Tyler!" boomed Dillon, he spat the last word 'Tyler' as if it was a horrible insult. "I will be back to kill you later, or One might."

I opened my mouth to talk but a table came flying straight at me and the world went black, I lay there listening to Angelique scream and felt thick liquid trickle down my face. This lasted minutes, hours, days I didn't know although Angelique had been taken away almost instantly. Then I smelt smoke and something snake-like slivered down my throat filling my lungs and choking me.

As Dillon strode out, the unconscious body of Angelique on his shoulder, he tossed a lit lighter over his shoulder. The wooden table it landed on instantly caught alight.

Kane stood one street away as something flammable in The *Holiday inn* caught fire and part of the building exploded, the windows all shattered and blew out on the bottom floor and the building's roof collapsed.

A fireman approached Kane and told him to leave quickly so that's what he did; he would continue searching for his cousin. He couldn't be dead.

The flames roared as an intense heat overwhelmed my systems and swirled through the lobby. I slowly opened my eyes and came to grips with the reality of searing hot fire destroying the lobby.

The mainly wooden interior was collapsing in on itself, support beams and chunks and ceiling tumbled down into the floor.

As I sat up I saw Lewis. He was unconscious amidst the flames; fire consumed his body as his skin melted. Conor and Jaden stood a few steps back as the orange licked Lewis, trying to figure out how to save him.

"He's gone," shouted Jaden over the sound of the buildings foundation breaking. "Go check Ollie, I'll check Joey."

Conor nodded as he jogged over to Ollie who has also just awoken. He was rubbing his hair that for once wasn't the reddest thing in the room. As Conor proceeded he dropped to the ground, thick black smoke entered his mouth and nostrils and colossal coughing fits shook his body.

Jaden ran over as Lewis sat up, still encased by fire. The ferocity of a dragon and the heat of a sun swirled up Lewis' sides but he just stood up. The skin that appeared to be permanently damaged was healing itself.

Lewis fixed eyes on me then dashed forward, scooping me up. Through the flames he ran, cradling me like a new born. He barrelled through the back door into an alley and dropped me.

"Stay!" he commanded, already back in the building. I choked and got back up as my lungs were filled with oxygen again.

Lewis returned this time gripping an ash layered Ollie. Closely following were Jaden and Conor.

The five of us gathered in a circle and took in a few deep breaths, thankful for being able to breath in something other than smoke.

"Now what?" asked Ollie. "We have to go somewhere else."

"We have to rescue Angelique," I answered. "That one eyed guy took her away."

"Angelique is dead," said Ollie. "No way she's alive now, W.S.I has her."

"They didn't kill her though," I said, pain in my voice. "She'll still be alive, W.S.I have her imprisoned somewhere."

"It would be suicide to go wherever she is."

"I agree with the ginger for once," nodded Jaden. "She's as good as dead."

"We can't give up, she's been kidnapped and we have to save her."

"She's probably in Portugal," grunted Conor, contributing to the conversation for the first time.

"Portugal why there?" I asked

"That's where most prisoners of W.S.I are sent, it's where you were heading to on the boat," he replied.

"And you know this how?"

"Because I worked for W.S.I," stated Conor.

I stuttered at this revelation of news. "S-So how can we know to trust you?" I asked.

"Well you used to work for W.S.I as well."

Before I could respond the hotels back door flung open again revealing the flames. A W.S.I henchman came tumbling out, drenched in fire and screaming.

Conor twirled and fired into his scalp, silencing him. The man twitched as the flames were dowsed by a jacket which Jaden threw on them.

"We need to move then," barked Lewis. The sound of fire engines screeched in the distance.

I noticed something peculiar about the dead agent as everyone jogged away. He had an I.D badge hung on his chest that vaguely resembled someone I knew. Me! The stern faced profile picture on the I.D card had several likenesses to me, such as the hair and eyes. I picked it up and

looked at the card that could get me into any
W.S.I base.

I also noticed that the man was wearing a
black jumpsuit, up either side of the jumpsuit ran
thin blue wires. If one wire was pulled a
parachute would be ejected, if the other was
pulled then the suit would expand and enable the
wearer to float in water. The suit also had
thermal pads stitched to the inside to keep warm
in the coldest conditions, could stop the impact
of low calibre bullets and was extremely
lightweight. I removed the jump that was still
intact, minus a few scorch marks, and rushed
over to my friends with a plan.

One watched through his scope as Joey Tyler
ran back to his group excited and explained his
plan. He had changed clothes since last time; he
was now wearing a jumpsuit, the sort Rico
supplied. One was wearing a similar jumpsuit
under his trench coat but his was more advanced
with dozens of extra features to protect him. For
starters if One was killed no one could remove

his suit without being shocked, only One could remove his suit.

One had the perfect shot to kill Joey Tyler. The ignorant billionaire, sorry ex-billionaire, had no idea he was being watched and would be dead within a second if he hadn't of been instructed otherwise since. There was a traitor in Joey's mist that would soon stab him in the back. One would just have to stick close and make sure that the traitor did not get any other ideas and if he failed One would put a bullet in both of their brains. The traitor looked up spotting One and looked him right in the eye. He couldn't have said something if he wanted to or else the trigger would be pulled and a bullet would smack between straight between his eyes.

Dillon had his pure one, the dark one was in the corner snivelling and crying.

"Why did you do this," sobbed Rico. He screamed as Dillon turned and smacked Rico in the jaw, there was a sickening crunch and blood bubble out between his cracked lips.

Rico curled up and cried, the power had tipped and now the leering man that usually struck fear into people's soul. Now he was crying, bleeding and urinating a little bit in a corner as an almost complete stranger missing an eye kicked him in the back. Each blow gave a cracking sound that satisfied Dillon.

It was all falling into place for Dillon, his master would rise and no one would stop him. The key was within Dillon's grasp he was just days away from reaching it and anyone who got in his way would be crushed like an ant under his boot.

I couldn't believe it had worked! The plan was extremely stupid and would have gotten us killed, if not for sheer dumb luck. With the money that Jaden had stolen we had got to the train station. After an hour journey to where Conor had said that a cargo train was departing from. We had gotten off where I had handcuffed the others and marched them to the train. I also put a black cap on to cover part of my face but I still looked like the man who died. With a few elbows to the others backs, a bit of charm and with the I.D card I had managed to bluff my way onto a cargo train stating that the others were my prisoners. Thankfully not a single person recognised me even though I was on their hit list, probably at the top. I only spoke to two people however and then I took the others straight to one of the storage carriages filled with crates full of ammunition and guns. Conor wanted to get his hands on the weapons but there was someone else in the carriage so I had to chain them to the walls.

The other man sat on a rusted fold chair smoking a cigar, billowing thick, vile smoke throughout the carriage. The stench stank and I choked on it as the slithers of smog coiled up my nose. The man was only about 30 and seemed physically fit due to W.S.I training but the heavy smoking had taking a toll on him. If it came down to strength the man could probably defeat everyone in the room, except maybe Lewis and Conor, but the man also looked slow. As if someone had sucked the stamina out of him and he would collapse after a short jog.

I sat in silence focused on the man's cigar.

"Don't smoke then kid?" said the man, not looking at me but keeping his gaze fixated at his cigar.

"Course not! Shut up!" spat Lewis, he had forgotten that he was imprisoned.

"Shut him up," grunted the man, taking a deep inhale then coughing. I just stood. "I said shut them up Joey do something."

I uncomfortably strode towards Lewis and punched him in the stomach. I knew it would not hurt Lewis but I still felt bad. Lewis pretended it hurt him as a gasp of air rapidly escaped his lungs.

"There you go kid."

Suddenly I realised something. "How did you know my name?" The fear in my voice was obvious and I instantly regretted asking the question because it made me come across as weak and afraid. My sweaty palms tried to reach for the pistol strapped to my left hip.

There was a bang and then a smouldering hole next to my head in a crate. The bullet was so close to my head that the man must have missed on purpose. He could have killed me without hesitation before I could have moved so I dropped my gun.

"There's a good boy," muttered the man, his gaze was still fixated on his cigar in one hand, and his other hand was occupied by the gun aimed at my chest. "You really think I wouldn't recognise you, you must be stupid, your number two on Dillon's hit list, second to only that bastard who has caused us a hell of a lot of trouble." He gestured to Lewis.

"Dillon's hit list?" asked Jaden apparently not bothered by the fact that I had a gun pointed to my head.

"Yeah didn't you hear? Old Rico kicked the bucket last night, died of a heart attack. A lot better than he deserved but that bastards gone now so people can sleep safely at night now. Except they can't. Somehow an unknown man on Rico's will was left the company. A ruthless scary man named Dillon Drake who's missing an eye. That bastard is twice as scary and has now changed the whole companies lay out.

Thousands of people out hunting you all across the country.

10 million for Lewis dead, 15 million for Joey alive. I got promoted to this taskforce. Me, Ruben Shapiro, just a runt in the lower levels of the operation barely able to hold a gun now I'm here."

"God I didn't ask for your life story. JEEZ!" said Jaden, once again forgetting the dire situation we were in.

Ruben took three strides forward and smacked Jaden in the jaw with his gun. There was a crack and blood ran out between his lips.

"AH SH-!" Lewis launched across the cart snapping the chains on the wall and sending crates flying everywhere. He smacked into Ruben and they both crashed through the sheet metal that divided this carriage and the next.

"Hey guys look up," grunted Ollie.

"Shut up Ollie," snapped Conor.

There was the sound of a struggle next door then Ruben's unconscious body was flung through the hole in the wall. One of his arms was completely bent backwards and the other had a stark white bone sticking out from the wrist.

119

"What did you do to him," I said the panic noticeable in my voice. Lewis didn't reply just panted and stared at Ruben, daring him to move. Which he obviously couldn't with his leg bent at such an angle. Blood flowed freely from his head, chest and legs.

"Guys look up!" shouted Ollie. That was when thick green gas filled the room.

Then it all went dark for me....Again.

15

One was not going to murder Joey Tyler now. Apparently he was too valuable to Mr Dillon's operation to be killed now. The final piece of the puzzle or some crap like that, One didn't care he just followed orders.

He was going to oversee the execution of Joey's fellow comrades. The four of them had caused a lot of trouble for the mission, the imbeciles would all still have a quick death, much better than they deserved.

Their execution was to be carried out by Dillon's top executioner, she had no name that anyone knew off and was simply referred to as 'her'. She was nice to One, didn't scream at him or call him a freak. She just smiled from under her huge black hood before she swung the sword that ended people.

They had even spoken once, suggested that they get a coffee sometime, before One got the chance he was shipped off to Bulgaria for a month. When he returned she was in China. It would be good to see her again.

No! One had to banish these thoughts from his mind, any woman was a distraction from work and a distraction would hinder his performance that could result in his and her death.

One just had to walk into the room where the four men were tied to chairs and make sure she cuts off all of their heads. Easy. The four men did deserve it, didn't they?

Of course they did! One needed to stop these incorrect thoughts, what was wrong with him today? It was the girl he had to ignore her then never see her after today that would be best, for everyone but him.

The four men were all tied to chairs, bloody and bruised, all their heads hung in shame; except for the blonde boy who was obviously unconscious. That boy had to be kept sedated now because he was too much of a risk to be conscious.

A fifth man was being held against the wall by two of Mr Drake's guards. There was a burlap sack stained with blood over his head and whimpering could be heard faintly from underneath.

She was stood behind the men tied to the chairs, a silver sparkling sword grasped firmly in her palm.

The room the execution would take place in was just another carriage at the back of this cargo train. One had got on the train at the last stop and would get off at the next in 15 minutes. After the execution.

The first person was to be executed, the small, ginger boy, One hadn't bothered to learn his name. The executioner took a step forward and rested her sword on her right shoulder. As the silver glistened in the light of a single light bulb illuminating the room beads of thick sweat rolled down the ginger boy's forehead. Everyone collectively held their breath in a pregnant moment, anticipating the execution as the ginger boy whimpered.

Then One felt the wind rush around him, an intense wave of heat burn across his face, a blistering pain that boiled down to his soul. One was flung down a hill through the gaping hole in the wall; he fell through bushes and shrubs. He tried to slow his fall but when he grabbed at something his wrist broke. One fell unconscious just as the train exploded above.

After we were knocked unconscious by gas we were dragged into another carriage. Everyone except me was seated on a chair in the room's centre. I was shackled to the wall and a burlap sack was thrown over my head as a woman entered the carriage. Lewis was still unconscious on the chair as they sedated him once again after the gas. However I could still hear the others and Ollie whimpered and footsteps crossed towards him. There was a seconds anxiety before Ollie would have been killed when the bang happened.

As the wave of fire destroyed part of the metal that made up the train was reduced to ashes my shackles broke. I collided with the ground and lay dazed, my head clanged on the floor as the world turned sideways, the train overturned and I tumbled through the shattered remains of the roof.

My vision was an unholy mess of red and orange and black, my hearing was non-existent, I couldn't hear the screech of metal tearing, the scream of agents as bullets tore into them, leaving now wounded or the sound of a boy calling my name.

My nose didn't smell the scent of burning flesh as it was overloaded with the scent of smoke.

All I felt were the hands that clutched my unresponsive body and dragged me away from the carnage. Away from my friends.

Lewis' eyes flew open as a fireball engulfed his body, his skin melted off in a second and his hair was burnt down to its roots, around him chaos had struck. Joey was nowhere to be seen but Ollie, Jaden and Conor were still chained to their seats.

With a cry of pain and a roar of encouragement Lewis kicked off of his chair, breaking the wood into kindling and dived at his friends. He scooped them up in one arm and propelled himself out of the hole in the train. A large chunk of metal feel from the ceiling and cut down Lewis' face, his eye was severed and his mouth torn open. The shock made Lewis let go and his friends landed in the bush.

As Lewis ran away and leapt up a bullet pierced his liver, it was an easy shot because there was no skin left to break.

Kane had thought blowing up a hole in the train would be a good idea; Joey was on the other side of the carriage so the blast would only kill his captors. However the blast was a lot larger than previously anticipated and radiated heats that melted the frameworks of the train. The entire vehicle had been destroyed by now. The explosive had been supplied to Kane by his lieutenant Jack who had also underestimated the sheer damage it would do.

Kane, Jack and the third man in the group, Will, had successfully completed their mission. Kane's cousin Joey was safe in the backseat of their hummer with only a few bruises and a burn mark on his ankle. The same couldn't be said for the remainder of the men Joey was travelling with who had evidently perished in the flames.

When Kane had seen Joey get on the train he had asked Jack and Will to help him stage a rescue.

"Where are we going?" asked Jack, he was sat in the passenger seat next to Will who was driving. His features were similar to that of Lewis's except he was significantly shorter and skinnier. Jack wore a simple black tracksuit with a bullet proof vest under his shirt that made him seem more bulky. His blonde hair was quite short and contained about half a pot of wax.

"We return to a hideout in Southern France," replied Kane, his voice full of edge.

"Then what?" questioned Will.

"I don't know."

They drove for an hour down country lanes; the air was silent and scared. No one certain of their next move. If Joey was important like Dillon made him out to be then there would already be a group of hunters scouring the country for him, ruthless and determined.

That didn't matter to Kane because he had his cousin back; he actually had a member of family. There was a person who shared genes with Kane and that made him happy.

Kane had never known any other family, his father had died when Kane he was a five years but old his memories of him where vague and he rarely was around his father.,his mother had never been mentioned. The only thing that could break his spell of happiness was the voice that came from next to him.

"Who the hell are you and what have you done?" I growled, I was curled up on the backseat of a car, occupied by three complete strangers. I lunged forward and grabbed the closest man's throat, entirely ignoring the searing pain in my ankle.

The man whose throat I grabbed jumped back and shouted, a short blonde boy in the front seat whirled round at a pace that would have put an Olympic runner to shame and levelled a pistol at my forehead.

"Let go or there will be a bullet in your brain before you can squeal," snarled the blonde boy.

"No need for," choked the man as I dug my thumbs into his throat. "I'm sure our friend Joey will let go."

Instinctively my grasp loosened and I reached for the car door, rattling the handle. Panic was overcoming me. Who was this? Another few people trying to kill me? And where were my friends?

"You'll find it's locked," grunted the driver, his back was turned to me but I could tell he was a large person with a bulky frame.

Despite being told this news I continued to attempt opening the door for another minute. After the exhaustion of the day had finally caught up with me I abandoned that and turned to the person sat next to me, weary of making a move towards him because of the trigger happy blonde perched on the edge of the passenger seat.

"Who are you?" I asked the boy next to me, he looked slightly like me but taller and skinnier with jet black hair and more defined cheeks.

"Legally, I'm Kane Cliffton," answered the man. "In reality I am Kane Tyler, my father was Mick Tyler."

For an awkward moment my brain froze trying to comprehend the new information, trying to figure out how this was possible, and then Kane continued.

"After my father died in unfortunate circumstances that involved, well you know you was there," said Kane, the slightest hint of sadness echoed through his voice. "When I was finally eighteen I wanted to know who I was so I started doing some digging. I read in an old newspaper about a Mick Tyler who had died in the same explosion that killed your parents. That man was my father however he called himself Mick Cliffton to protect me from something." Whilst recounting this story a few stray tears filled Kane's eyes. "It didn't take a genius to figure out the link between you and Mick, him being your Uncle, and I figured you were my cousin."

"But, but how did you find me?" I stuttered, all of the facts Kane had told me trying to fit them in a logical order.

"You're not hard to find," chuckled the bulky driver.

"Shut up Will let me finish," snapped Kane. "I managed to get a job at W.S.I, security personnel; I got onto the train and rescued you."

"What about the people I was with!" I spat, hoping against hope they were alive.

"They are more than likely dead now," muttered the blonde boy. "The explosion I set off was much larger than expected, you was against the far wall so that's how you survived."

"You monsters!" I shouted. "How could you do that?" Once again I lunged at Kane at grabbed his neck, this time with full intent of killing someone.

"Joey stop it!" bellowed Kane, "If we hadn't of blown up the train they would have been executed anyway." My fingers just tightened, this man killed Lewis. "Jack help!"

The blonde boy leapt over his seat with athletic grace and connected his fists with my chest, then he grabbed my wrists overpowering me instantly and pinned my body back.

"You need to calm down," said Jack, I attempted to struggle against his powerful grip but it was futile, Jack completely overpowered me.

"Listen your alive that's what matters, and If it makes you feel better I'm terribly sorry for your loss," muttered Kane.

"Alive," I said as calmly as possible in short raspy breathes. "On the outside maybe, barely. On the inside no, everything I have is gone, the few people left in my life are now just bones and ashes."

"You have family now," said Kane, my words had shocked him and this was not the response he had expected.

I did not answer because my mind was racing over the thoughts, Ollie was dead, Jaden was dead, Conor was dead and Lewis was dead. No! That didn't sound correct, Lewis could survive worse than an explosion, it would take a bloody nuke to stop him.

"He's not dead!" I exclaimed. Kane and Jack stared at me dumbfounded. "Lewis must still be alive, probably injured the bomb site, he couldn't have been killed by that we must go back."

"We can't return," stated Will, "Too risky and too far now."

"How could I forget?" I shouted, slapping my forehead in frustration. "Angelique is at the base, that's why we were going there in the first place. Now it is imperative we go back."

"I said no and that's final," stated Kane.

After twenty minutes of arguing and me attempting to strangle Kane twice more without success Will finally turned the car around and we began a silent two hour journey towards where Lewis should be.

Lewis awoke in a puddle of blood, he had been unconscious for three hours and thirty four minutes, somehow the internal clock of his body knew that. His skin had entirely grown back by now; his flesh was pink, raw and still slightly sore. However it had returned without a hitch. The hole in Lewis' torso that had pierced his Liver had also been completely filled in. Despite being fully healed Lewis could not move, his legs and arms were fixed in place, only Lewis' neck would move side to side. That's when he noticed the men surrounding him; four men in black uniforms had strapped him to a stretcher with thick metal chains that felt like they weighed a tonne.

"We've got the boy now," smiled Alonzo. "Shame it cost the lives of everyone else on the train. Never mind who cares."

Behind Alonzo another man writhed on a stretcher but he was not chained down.

"You three take this one," barked Alonzo, pointing at three of the men surrounding Lewis. "You and I will carry back Mr Shapiro here."

"AHHHHHHH!" a war cry echoed out and three men dived out from the bushes, they ran down a slight incline and Lewis now realised he had caused a crater when he had landed.

Before Ollie, Jaden and Conor had reached Lewis they had all been tasered apart from Ollie who had been shot at and narrowly missed. All three dropped to the ground and all three were scooped up by Alonzo's henchmen.

"Let's get these men back to base in Portugal, pick up one each," ordered Alonzo. "Come on let's move!"

One awoke relatively unharmed in some shrubbery and the first thing that crossed his mind was her, the executioner. He was wishing she was ok, that the explosion had barely harmed her but he knew this couldn't be true, it was a miracle that he was in once piece and the chances of them both being alive was impossible, insane to even believe there was a chance. Anyway it was good she was dead, no more distractions to One's work, nothing to get hung up and no one that could ever be used against him, he was a freak, and freaks don't need love.

"So you're finally awake then," grunted Dillon. "Help him up Thea."

One looked up and Dillon Drake was standing over him standing next to him was the stupid executioner and despite feeling saddened that there was someone to use against him One felt happy. Thea? That must be her name.

"You sustained a rather large injury, you need to heal quickly though you have another mission," Dillon's voice was as rough as gravel and showed no sympathy for his injured comrade.

"What?" muttered One. The executioner, Thea, nodded at One's abdomen.

Before he passed out the last thing he saw was the huge piece of shrapnel that stuck out of his lower intestines at an abnormal angle.

16

Me, Jack, Will and Kane had reached the wreckage after three hours and found nothing. The rubble was extensive, most of it unrecognisable charred ashes, an extensive search revealed only four bodies, none of which were my friends.

There was one more body however they may have been someone I know but the face had been burnt so badly that it had become a disfigured puddle of melted flesh and bone.

"We're not going to find anything," stated Jack, he was clearly bored by this by now.

"Have patience Jack, that is one virtue you clearly do not possess," said Will, he was busy picking through gigantic sheets of black metal. He drew back a particularly large sheet and found something. "Look at this!" called Will.

"I'm coming over," replied Kane. He jogged over and took a long look at Will's discovery. "That's disgusting."

What lay by our feet was another body, partially intact. This unfortunate employee of W.S.I had survived the initial explosion but then been flung out of the carriage and caught his chest on the metal. The large sharp piece of wreckage had pierced his ribcage then proceeded to tear down, causing a gaping rip in the man's abdomen causing his insides to spill out around him.

"That's lovely isn't Joe?" Jack grinned elbowing me discreetly.

"It's Joey," I answered.

"Same thing. Why are you annoyed?" snorted Jack.

"Because you may have killed the only friends I had left in the world," I growled. "That's why."

"Most likely they were captured by whoever survived the explosion and taken to Portugal were the train was going to In the first place," said Jack.

"When did you come up with that idea?" asked Kane, seemingly the slightest bit irritated with Jack.

"When we got here," admitted Jack.

"So why are you only telling us," huffed Will, his answer was only a Jack. "You know Jack sometimes you say something and I think you are genius but my opinion of you always somehow reverts back to me thinking you are an absolute moron."

"So are going to Portugal now?" I asked.

"We should make one stop on the way, I know a place that could be useful," replied Kane.

We returned to the car and after another very long and very silent drive reached our destination.

The place in question was a small abandoned warehouse on the border between France and Spain. It was a dismal, rusty shelter that stuck out in the field like a sore thumb. The warehouse was ugly and looked to be at the stage of collapsing any second now.

"What is this piece of crap," I scoffed. "The roof will cave in on us if we step foot in there."

"What's in there is very valuable indeed actually cousin," chuckled Kane and then he strode in ahead of me.

"I haven't given you permission to call me that yet," I grumbled and jogged in after him.

The inside was just as much of a mess as the outside, boxes were strewn out across the ground, stray wires hung from the ceiling and rusty puddles gathered in the corner.

Kane reached into the closest box and drew out a sniper rifle, it was a bulky, black carbon rifle with a built in magnified scope that had a thermal feature. In the grip was a sliding slot that a bipod could be withdrawn from.

"Pretty neat right?" said Kane; his affection for this weapon was obvious.

"I guess," I shrugged.

"This my absolute favourite," grinned Jack, in his hands he was holding a thin metal stick that glistened in reflection, it was hollowed out and the inside was filled with a creamy goo. There were two buttons on it, one red one green. "This is great." Jack spun on his toes and pointed the stick at a tattered target hanging from the ceiling; he held the green button and the goo sprayed over the target. The target began hissing, then sizzling. The entire fabric melted, a few remains on the ground. Jack clicked the red button and whatever was left exploded, a black smudge was all that was left behind.

"The damage to a body would just be, wow" giggle Jack, revelling at the slight sprinkling of ash on the ground.

"That causes too much carnage," snorted Will. "A simple quick kill would be more effective." Will put on a black leather glove and pointed it in Jack's direction. His fingers were spread out wide. "Active Code Storm." He said very clearly then Will clenched his fist firing a blade from his wrist, it struck the box closest to me and quivered for a few seconds.

"I'm not really a fan," I admitted.

"I'm not finished," replied Will. "Mode 2" A very long silver blade slid from the palm of his hand, a sharp sword that I did not want to get on the wrong end of. Finally Will said "Mode 3" The glove lit up blue, it emitted a buzzing noise and smalls sparks flew around the fingertips.

"Up to 5000 volts this will go," smirked Will. "It'll fry your brains out."

"So go ahead Joey," said Kane. "Take your pick of any weapon, on me."

At random I selected a box and withdrew a heavy bullet proof vest; it was thicker than my skull and would serve great protection. This was my favourite thing in here.

In another box was a black motorcycle helmet with a red visor, I picked up the sphere and placed it over my head, it fit perfectly. The cushioned inside would protect my head from impact and felt very comfortable.

Finally I picked up a riot shield that lay face down a few feet away, it was dusty and had sustained a few dents but I'd rather use this than a gun. Plus at the press of the button a small blade fired from the front but that was one use only. Kane made it clear only to use in in emergencies.

Despite my unwillingness to wield a gun in a fight I slotted a small pistol in a holster attached to the back of my shield, it would be a last resort only. Most likely to use on myself if the I was captured and all others killed.

"Are you ready?" asked Kane, his gun was stood vertically on the floor and he was slowly spinning it.

"Yes," I muttered. "I just hope Lewis is there." But in my head I knew the chances of that were miniscule, but I had to hope.

Jaden Snow opened his eyes to be greeted by the ugly face of Alonzo, his shattered grin chilled Jaden.

"Your finally awake Mr Snow," stated Alonzo, his demeanour was cool and calm. Then something flicked inside Alonzo. Before Jaden could open his mouth Alonzo picked up the chair Jaden was chained to and flung it across the room.

Jaden skidded across the floor and his head clattered against the wall with a deafening bang. Jaden was instantly dizzied and his vision turned sideways. A thin trickle of thick blood flowed from Jaden's brow and a drop of the scarlet substance fell into his eye, reddening Jaden's vision.

"You have one attempt to answer this correctly Mr Snow," snarled Alonzo.

Jaden's mouth opened and a gargled version of something that sounded like 'shove it up your arse' came out along with a little bit of blood.

Alonzo marched two steps forward and kicked Jaden in the stomach.

"ARGGH!" He instantly recoiled at the pain of being hit and curled up into a ball.

"Will you tell me now Mr Snow?" asked Alonzo, a wide smile was spreading across his face. Jaden looked up and flipped him the finger. "Very well," said Alonzo, his foot connected with Jaden's chin followed by a satisfactory crunch. "Bring in the next one," called Alonzo as Jaden was dragged out of the room.

Jaden was face down whilst he was dragged but he felt that he turned two corners before being flung into his cell like a rag doll. He was now useless to Dillon so Jaden was uncertain of how much longer he would be kept alive. Most likely they would execute him after Ollie and Conor had been interrogated, trying to extract as much information as possible. But Dillon was beating a dead horse; none of them knew where

Joey was and even if they did no one would reveal anything.

Except maybe Ollie, Jaden did not trust Ollie. He had barely known the boy a week and he had spoken to him about once. Jaden didn't trust Lewis much either, yet he liked him. There was something about Lewis that reminded Jaden of himself. Lewis had a childish nature, however not afraid to break a bone like some sort of criminal.

Jaden wasn't a petty criminal though. Jaden Snow was a master thief.

The interrogators kicked and beat Ollie but like Jaden they received no new information. Ollie honestly didn't know where Joey had gone but if he did know he wasn't sure if he would rat him out or not. Dillon's men were possibly going to murder Ollie today so he was not sure what extents he would go to for his own safety.

Perhaps if the time came Ollie would sell out Joey for his life, perhaps.

The silver Audi zipped down the Portuguese coastal road, the cool ocean breeze rushing in through the windows. The car was travelling at 90mph but at 1 in the morning there is scarcely a soul about. If by chance the car did come across someone the driver was apt behind the wheel and could easily avoid the accident.

Because being pulled over was the last thing the four of us wanted was to be pulled over. The boot of Kane's newly bought Audi was stocked full of weapons and explosives that would arouse the suspicion of even the dumbest policeman.

"Only about a thirty minute drive to where the base should be," confirmed Will from the front seat. Once again I was in the back seat with Kane and Jack was sat upfront.

"Ok just don't damage the car or you're paying," warned Kane. Despite having only bought this car yesterday ago Kane treated it as his own child. The four of us stopped at a large dealership back in Paris where Kane had bought this beauty using the W.S.I payroll. The manager did not seem to mind this as he was still getting paid either way. So now my cousin was the proud owner of a snow white Audi.

I told him it would stick out, be too obvious, Kane just loved his car too much to let it go.

"If they are there," Jack said not directly speaking to anyone. "I'm going to blow up so many people. And if Dillon's there I'm spray this explosive putty all over his face." Jack had the putty sprayer, as Jack had dubbed it himself, in-betweens his fingers and was rolling it about, feeling the weight. Everyone had all of their weapons on them now except me who had to store my riot shield in the boot because there was no room where we were sitting. Especially since Kane's sniper rifle was laid out across both of our laps.

As we travelled a thought crossed my mind, Lewis is sort of a spirit stored in my locket. He had always been there and only exited the locket when he was most needed. I wondered if there was any way to return Lewis back into the locket if this was ever over. Lewis was a trouble magnet, wherever he went Dillon or Rico or whoever would be in charge next would find him. They would hunt Lewis globally like they have been doing, not stopping for anything with no sense of remorse.

Maybe if Lewis was gone then people would be safer, W.S.I would have no reason to hunt me. Of course they couldn't let me live, I'd go to the public. Evidently either path I took ended in the death of me and possibly many others.

"So how do we plan to get into the base?" asked Will. "Are we just gonna roll up in our Audi and ask to enter, seems a bit stupid really."

"We go in a shoot all them all down before anyone gets the chance to react," said Jack. "Use the element of surprise and blow their faces off."

"That's ridiculous Jack they outnumber us about five hundred to one," said Will. "Can you think of something smart for once. Kane what are we doing?"

"Exactly what Jack said."

The Audi tore through the maze field tossing up bits of corn under its back wheels. The entire facility was surrounded by maze fields to keep it hidden, the downside to this was that the six foot tall corn would also conceal any approaching enemies. The noise of the Audi would have given us away if not for the constant noise of trucks circling the perimeter and the hustle of people.

Kane had told us that all of the bases not built in the last five years were nearly identical; they all followed the new layout so Kane knew where the holding cells most likely were.

However there was one part of the base that was not listed on any maps, there was a giant bio dome that looked exactly identical to a giant golf ball cut in half. None of us knew what was in there but the dome was on none of our minds as we raced across the tarmac at 90mph and knocked over half a dozen men.

17

The helicopter touched down in the dusty Cairo desert as the blades whipped up a sandstorm around the hull of the chopper. It landed gracefully just as the last ray of sun sunk below the horizon and plunged the simple landscape into almost absolute darkness.

After a second of deafening silence the beaming headlights attached the helicopters roof lit up and engulfed the dessert with blinding streaks of light. As the glowing lights flicked on four heavily armed people stepped out of the chopper.

The four people that had just touched down in Cairo were Dillon Drake, One, The executioner and Alonzo.

All of them except for Dillon had been scattered apart due to the explosion on the train but once everyone had regained their senses they managed to find each other.

They had also found all of the wretched boys who had disrupted their plans except for Joey Tyler himself who was missing; the few they had found were shipped ahead to the base in Portugal were they were originally destined to go along with those injured in the explosion.

The identities of the group who had initiated the explosion were still unknown but Dillon suspected it was an inside job.

"Ok bring them out!" bellowed Dillon, his single creepy eye surveyed the surroundings and focused on the majestic Sphinx, built thousands of years ago and still standing. Of course the beast was still standing, it encased the greatest power ever, and it was built to withstand hundreds of thousands of years.

Behind the four of them two more heavily armed men appeared each dragging a body with their faces covered by a burlap sack.

"Excellent," cooed Dillon. "There's only one more we need now."

"But sir," interrupted Alonzo. "We have no idea where Mr Tyler is, and even if we find him unless Lewis is killed it won't work."

Dillon swirled around on his toes at an impossible speed and stared down Alonzo with a look as cold as ice, his single evil eye looked straight through Alonzo.

Inside his chest Alonzo felt his heart ice over and a tingle rise up his spine, his entire body was paralysed, he couldn't have ran if he wanted to.

"I am with you brothers," mouthed Alonzo, he closed his eyes realising that Dillon would kill him. Then the air rushed, everything swirled, wind flew through Alonzo's ears and the CRASH!!!

The Spaniard was hurtled across the dessert by an arm with unmeasurable strength and collided into a sand dune sending tiny chunks of rock shooting off in every possible direction and whipping up a sand cloud.

Alonzo's back hurt, his arms hurt, his legs hurt and his head hurt but Dillon had left him alive, that was a lot better than many before had got.

"They will come to me!" bellowed Dillon.
"We have her! The boy Joey will come here to save her!"

Of the two men carrying the dragging the body's one was having more difficulty because his hostage was rapidly shaking and screaming. Whoever was underneath the sac shook and tossed trying the break free but the man's grip was too strong.

"How do you know he will come for her, is she even important sir?" One questioned as quietly as possible, Dillon still heard it.

Once again a boiling rage shot up through Dillon, all of his instincts wanting to murder One right now, however the rage quickly quelled, One was too valuable. He could have probably been killed by a simple punch and One was still recovering from his stomach surgery in which the shrapnel had to be removed. He was fine now though.

"Uncover her," ordered Dillon. The burlap sack covering the face of the struggling body was pulled off and blonde hair spilled out from underneath like threads of gold.

"You're right Joey may come," muttered Angelique, her blues eyes flooded with tears. "But he will kill you."

"Do you have faith in Joey?" chuckled Dillon, crouching down so he was level with the kneeling Angelique.

"Complete," said Angelique.

"That's amusing," said Dillon with the faintest of smiles. "The boy will fail you, he will die along with you and I will reign supreme."

Angelique took in a deep breath and then hawked up a wad of spit directly into Dillon's empty eye socket.

Dillon raised his right hand and brought it down across Angelique's face leaving a large red welt, she let out a cry of pain and collapsed into the sand.

"We will come to us my lord," whispered Dillon, casting a glaze to the sky. "The boy will arrive soon."

In the back of Dillon's skull he heard the smallest of voices, a raspy voice like a thousand claws being dragged down a chalkboard. Two words that sent a jolt through Dillon.

"He better."

18

The car zipped along faster than expected and barrelled into a shocked security guard; the unfortunate man spun towards the car, gun in hands, and fired a spray of death at the car. Only two bullets managed to leave the gun, both missed, before the hood of the Audi struck. The security guard was flattened with a sickening squelch that made me gag whilst a torrent of blood exploded across the windscreen.

"We can't see!" shouted Jack, his voice filled with unravelled joy. "I'm gonna jump out!"

"Wait!" ordered Kane. "We're going too fast!" He reached forward but was too slow before Jack leapt out of the car.

The blonde maniac dove gracefully through the air, a submachine gun clasped in his right hand, blazing bullets across the perimeter.

His small body smacked into a surprised guard, from afar I recognised this man as one of the people who was overseeing Lewis' execution. Jack gripped the man's shirt and used him as a makeshift sled, the man's body sliding across the concrete leaving a trail of thick blood. If Jack had not landed on this man he would surely be dead. Instead the guard was dead, fortunately for him he had died almost straight away when his skull had cracked against the ground so he couldn't feel the agony he should be feeling right now.

When the sliding body finally came to a halt due to friction Jack rolled off and starting shooting at anything that moved, his fingers worked excessively, raining death upon all who came close to him.

However Jack had now lost the element of surprise and it only took a few seconds for everyone around to snap to action and fire at Jack who was forced to take cover behind an empty truck.

The few people who were not near Jack drew their firearms from their holsters and unleashed hell on the car I was in.

"Get down!" screamed Will as the three of us instinctively dropped to the pristine car floor, dozens of metal bullets zoomed over our heads as all of the cars windows including the front and back windscreen shattered into a million tiny glass fragments. The glass rained down onto the back of my neck and when I used my hands to cover it they were dotted with a thousand miniscule cuts and slashes.

All around us the men and women firing at us advanced, creating a tight circle around the car and never stopping their shooting unless to reload, and still the gun wielders came closer until they were half a foot away from the car and the firing at us stopped. Most people now abandoned their guns due to lack of ammo but there were still four or five loaded pistols pointed at us.

"Joey Tyler himself," said one of the men still holding a gun as he leant through where the window used to be with a yellow toothed grin. "I think Dillon will be particularly happy when I execute you, won't he?" The man levelled his pistol with my forehead, his finger just itching to shoot.

"You can't kill him," piped up a woman from behind, she looked only young, in her early twenties maybe. "Kill the others but Dillon wants Joey."

"Shut up Charlotte!" snapped the man, he turned to face Charlotte taking his eyes off of the car for half a second and that was all Will needed.

"Brace yourselves," Will screamed as he slammed his hand on the accelerator and the car shot forward out of the circle, there was a screech of tires and the smell of burning rubber whilst Will reached up from the floor and sharply turned the wheel to right at a sharp angle. Men and women dove out of the way as the car continued forward at an unrelenting speed. Suddenly the giant golf dome was right in front of them, there was a crunch of metal and the world spun and a woman was screaming. The car dipped sickeningly and hit something and the airbags rushed out, knocking Will's head back. My body floated in the air for a split second but before I knew it I fell flat onto the ceiling of the now upturned car. The engine was running but we were no longer moving.

I went for the release catch on the door but it didn't work, the door was stuck and my feet were wet. Why were my feet wet? The car had dipped into what appeared to be a short flowing stream that was slowing the car through the windows. It rushed through at an increasing pace soaking my body armour; however the gushing torrent wasn't strong enough to stop me dragging my bruised body out onto the river bank.

I collapsed into the waist high grass and filled my lungs with as much air as possible, I took huge gasping breathes before leaning forward, intending to help Kane and Will out of the car.

Before I got the opportunity to do this there was a clang next to me and a looming shadow hung over me.

"Wake up lazy," barked Kane, jolting me into action. He had just dropped my riot shield next to me. "Pick it up!"

"It's so nice here," I whispered serenely, I had not been listening to Kane and was taking in the surroundings. Inside the dome we had crashed into was a lush green meadow with a turquoise blue stream flowing through the middle, the field was plagued with bright, colourful flowers, every colour the brain could comprehend was here in front of me. This small indoor Eden was a perfectly peaceful paradise that drew me away from the fighting outside making me want to do nothing more than lay down and watch the world go by.

This was until Jack dived through the hole in the reinforced glass that let the fighting and violence of the outside world into the little dome like a tiny hole on a submarine can bring hundreds of gallons of water crashing in and destroying everything inside.

Jack released a cry of happiness as he splashed down into the river followed by the bangs of bullets and the whizzing of death flying by.

"Cover me!" bellowed Jack as he crouched in the river mud to reload his machine gun, as he flicked the catch and dropped the empty magazine in the water a soaking wet Will raised his dual pistols unleashing a frenzy of fire upon the advancing enemies.

"Get up Joey," screamed someone; I had no idea who commanded this because I could barely here them over the gunfire. I hooked my left arm through the strap of my shield and stood up as a few bullets pinged off of the metal protecting me, inside my chest I felt my heart rate quicken to such a rate that it felt like it would explode from my chest. I withdrew a pistol from my belt as the cold hard truth slapped me like a brick wall; there was no way of getting out of this. If I survived this ordeal here, if I rescued Lewis I would still be hunted, Dillon would find me and kill me.

I knew this was true but the part of my brain that responded to reason and logic had shut down, I was now operating on pure instinct, the raw animal side of my brain that wanted nothing but to survive had kicked in rendering all of my knowledge useless, despite the ache in my arm and the dead weight feeling of the gun in my hand I continued to shoot because when it came to the inside all humans were the same, animals.

The pounding in my chest was now completely in sync with the thunder clap of the gun in my hand, each shot whizzed forward at an astronomical speed but I was unsure whether I ever actually hit a target or my gun fire was just keeping the enemies at bay.

As my right index finger clicked the trigger for a final time a haunting noise echoed through me, the sound that indicated I was out of ammo. I did not have the stomach to use my sword to survive, I would have to look at the person before plunging my blade into them and it killed me to think that the bodies scattered around were real people as well, probably with families and lives and people who would miss them.

"I'm out of bullets," I shouted so loud that my voice went hoarse and I was still barely heard over the sound of the battle.

"Take cover then!" replied Kane. He was lying in the thick grass with his sniper rifle picking off anyone who got too brave or came too close. Every time Kane pulled the trigger he winced at knowing the fact he had just killed someone. Yes, that person had been trying to kill him but almost every person would stick in his mind for a very long time.

Will was taking a more reserved approach having managed to sneak around the other side of the enemies keeping close to the domes huge walls. Now he was circling the edge and using to gloves to shock as many people as possible, I would have preferred his weapon to a gun because the electricity did not kill only render unconscious. Occasionally someone would spot Will and turn to shoot but would find a tiny blade lodged in their throat before their finger reached the trigger.

I dived behind the Audi just as Jack screams "Get down!" A particularly courageous or stupid man had charged straight forward, Jack unclipped one of the tubes from his belt and sprayed the entirety of its explosive gel over the man's face, as the acid started to burn through his skull Jack unclipped another tube and sprayed its contents on the man's chest. For a few seconds there was absolute silence and a halt in silence as the man screamed in a pitch that made me want to tear my ears clean off and bury them six foot underground.

"HEUUUUS!" screamed the man, presumably he wanted to say help but his lips and tongue had melted away.

"Sorry," whispered Jack as he gripped the man by the scruff of his neck and using amazing strength tossed him towards the guards that had been shooting at us. The man tumbled into a few people as he tried to scream but instead a strangled gurgle emerged from his throat.

Next Jack gripped the two empty tubes, one held in each hand, then clicked the second on each.

"Oh shi-," said Kane in slight awe before rolling over so he splashed down in the river. Simultaneously with Kane, Will mouth something inaudible and ran the other way away from the dome.

I realised what was happening a nano-second before the explosion rocked out across the entirety of the base. A quarter of a tubes worth of the explosive gel had the power of a frag grenade, Jack had used eight times that amount.

A mushroom cloud of fire rose up obliterating everyone in its radius, the explosion made the ground vibrate at a force that sent me flying back into a flower patch, chunks of thin glass as long as my body rained from the sky and shattered upon impact with the ground.

Jaden sat in the corner of his cell thinking over the events of the past week, how he had got himself in this situation. He had stolen a piece of paper from Rico, that's all some paper. A script with weird text on it about sand and souls, mostly confusing things. Ollie had told him that he'd found the script in a cave in Southern China, he'd refused to give it up to Rico, he never said why just that it would allow Rico to do great evil. Jaden didn't believe that, it was just a scrap of paper, however it was important enough to cost Ollie one of his fingers.

Conor had not brought himself into this situation either, Jaden had brought his best friend into all of this, probably cost him his life. Conor would never see his family again; if they were found.

Jaden knew he would end up in a prison eventually; he had stolen the crown jewels but Jaden had not expected to be in a tiny cell in the middle of nowhere with no one knowing what he had done in life.

"Why am I here?" Jaden prayed silently, his thoughts were then violently interrupted by an eruption of fire and noise outside. Jaden shot up and looked out of his barred cell window towards the echo dome where a ball of fire had spread then quickly dissipated leaving a crater, a lot of smoke and many corpses.

My vision was blurred by the waves of rolling smoke that drifted across the field, my ears rung replaying the sound of the explosion and my nose wanted to disappear from the foul stench of burning flesh and ash.

My mouth gagged on smoke, I choked on the aroma of death as I wandered round aimlessly through the grass until finally, finally the smoke cleared.

The sight in my eyes slowly returned to normal and the ringing bells stopped in my left ear, my right may have been damaged beyond repair.

When the black finally shifted I saw devastation, a small crater about the size of a tennis court with a dozen mangled and disfigured corpses littered around the rubble and scorch marks. Will was striding back towards us, eyeing up every single body individually, making sure none were moving and putting a bullet in the ones that did.

Whilst Kane jogged over to Will, Jack was weighing up another one of the explosive gel cylinders in his hands, the urge to use it again almost bursting through his skin.

"Excuse me who are?" said a soft feminine voice as someone tapped me on the shoulder. I whirled around, holding up my shield ready for combat, only to see a young woman cradling a baby in her arms.

She was of average height with considerably defined cheeks and strawberry blonde hair that flowed down to her chest like liquid gold.

"Who are you?" I asked; confused upon meeting a stranger that wasn't pointing a gun at me.

"I'm not sure," the woman chirped, she screwed up her face and tried her hardest to remember who she was. "I might be named Maisie? Is my name Maisie?" She asked.

"I don't know," I said.

"Then it is Maisie, I'm sure of it. I think."

From the river bank a very muddy Jack sprinted through the now ruined meadow towards me. He ran past knee high grass that had been consumed by fire, orange flames; this small paradise was now ravaged by bullet holes and rubble causing it to lose all sense of perfection.

"Joey!" called out Jack. "Are you OK? Where's Kane?"

"Oh goodie," squealed Maisie. "Another friend, George and I don't get many people visit here." I assumed George was the baby she was cradling that made soft cooing noises every few seconds.

"Who are you," growled Jack, from his waistband he whipped out a pistol and held it to Maisie's face.

"I don't think she's a threat Jack," I snapped. "I think she's a prisoner."

"Is that a boomerang?" asked Maisie, stroking the guns barrel with her forefinger.

"I think you're right," grunted Jack and placed the pistol back in his waistband. "So what did you do to W.S.I to make them kidnap you then?"

"Pardon?" asked Maisie.

"You were kidnapped right?"

"I'm not sure."

"How are you not sure?"

"Some men came to my house one day and took him away then I woke up here."

"Hold on, I'm confused," I said.

"So you were kidnapped," stated Jack.

"I'm not sure."

"Who is the 'him' that was taken away?" asked Jack, irritation was rising in his voice.

"You said they took him away," I said.

"Oh yeah, my husband," said Maisie, a smile spread across her face. "He told me he would come back and save me so I'm waiting."

Before any more questions could be asked Kane crawled came barrelling through towards us closely pursued by a man clutching a jagged knife. Kane was unarmed.

"Shoot him!" shouted Kane from about a hundred metres away but his voice was gurgled as he coughed. The man in came extremely close to Kane and dived head first, spittle flying from his mouth. The left side of his face was coated in blood and one of his eyes was badly damaged

168

beyond repair. He had obviously been injured in the explosion and the adrenalin meant the pain had not kicked in yet.

Kane and the man crashed into the ground, however a nanosecond before they impacted there was a deafening bang that left Kane panting on the ground with a dead body lain across his torso. Blood seeped from the body's head across Kane's chest.

"Next time please shoot him a bit quicker," said Kane as he rolled the corpse off of him and rapidly stood up.

"You panicking is fun," smirked Jack.

"Who's he?" asked Maisie, pointing a finger at the bloodied Kane. She did not seem fazed at all by the dead man or the disturbing amount of blood smothering Kane. "And what happened to my field? Is my husband here to rescue me?" The idea of that sent joy through Maisie and even her baby giggled a little bit.

"Your husband isn't with us," Kane stated blatantly.

"Oh," Maisie sounded deflated. "Are you sure he's not here?"

"Maybe," shrugged Kane. "He could be here in a cell somewhere but he's not with us."

As Maisie was speaking one of the supposedly dead enemies had survived the explosion and from the ground he raised his gun.

Kane turned on his heels hearing a slight noise, his gun however was out of ammo, Jack had used his last shot saving Kane before and the metal cylinders in his belt would take too long to use.

The man on the floor was missing his legs but still managed a menacing grin as he went pulled his finger back, he never got the chance to do so as a four inch dart impaled the back of his neck, he made a sound like a bath being emptied as blood slipped over his lower lip then collapsed.

Ten feet behind the now dead man stood Will, his right gloved hand extended and the finger tips lit up green to indicate that the dart feature was active, blue light meant that it would emit electricity whenever it came into contact with anything and no light meant it was deactivated.

"I do prove useful sometimes," smirked Will. "I just saved your life." Kane marched across the field and picked up a discarded gun that he pointed at Will's forehead. After a tense moment he slid the gun inside his waistband.

"And now I don't owe you any favours, I saved your life," said Kane.

"How?" asked Will.

"I decided not to shoot you, if I hadn't of done that you would have died so I saved your life."

"That's ridiculous."

"You're ridiculous."

"You didn't save my life."

Kane swivelled on the balls of his feet. "Did I save his life Jack?"

"Um not really," answered Jack.

"Whatever," muttered Kane. "As I outrank both of you I deem that I did."

Will and Jack did not argue after that both knowing Kane was too stubborn to admit he was wrong. Having not known Kane very well I thought he was joking.

"Can he hurry up?" I urged. "We're wasting time and people will be arriving soon, and explosion doesn't generally go unnoticed in a private military base."

Only two hundred metres from where I was Lewis was held in secure metal room surrounded by one-way mirrors and almost impenetrable steel. A violent explosion rocked Lewis out of his sedated sleep, and he sat up in the blink of an eye.

Lewis' arms were strapped to his sides by a strait Jacket modified with metal chains and hooks; however the extra effort was useless because Lewis managed to tear the entire Jacket in half from inside in two seconds. The fabric and steel fell to the floor with a clang allowing Lewis' arms free and fro him to explore his cell.

In the top left corner there was a tiny camera monitoring all of Lewis' movements bolted to the wall by titanium clamps. Lewis strode towards the camera and simply plucked it off of the wall then crushed it in his fist with minimal effort.

The entire cube of a room was completely unfurnished and relatively cramped; it was only the mirrors lined along the walls that created the illusion of space. On the other side of the mirror behind him Lewis picked up the faintest of whispering that would have been impossible to hear by any human. Lewis wasn't human as far as others were concerned him, something about him was different to the everyday person. There was one other person who could compete with Lewis in strength and speed but that individual was locked away for centuries to come, as far as Lewis knew.

As the whispering continued behind the mirror Lewis walked the opposite way, the glass and metal were supposedly unbreakable but Lewis was confident in his abilities.

He took two huge steps forward, his eyes fixed on the mirror ahead, the people hidden behind a different mirror behind him were certain he was unaware of their presence. They were wrong.

Lewis stretched his arms then kicked both of his legs against the mirror in front of him, the shards instantly shattered and the force of his kick launched his light body across the width of the room and straight through the apparently unbreakable mirror, millions of tiny glass fragments rained to the ground as Lewis shot through the air directly into the three very surprised workers that had been watching him. The surprise on their face was obvious as Lewis knocked every single person off of their chairs.

Lewis landed gracefully on the balls of his feet and proceeded to walk out of the room.

Outside the sound of gunfire and explosions had halted, Lewis could hear a few solemn footsteps and the voice of a woman, it was a voice he did not recognise. However Lewis' super hearing enabled him to recognise another voice even from far away, it was Joey's voice, and he sounded relatively unharmed.

He broke out into a sprint down the featureless grey corridor and rounded a corner towards where Joey's voice was coming from.

"I'm coming Joey," he muttered as his speed exceeded that of an Olympic runner, unfortunately before he knew what was happening there was a deafening bang that exploded down the long corridors like a grenade. Lewis stopped and peered down at the gaping hole that had revealed itself in his torso, the hole went straight through Lewis' entrails and you could clearly see a man holding a shotgun through the hole.

Lewis pivoted round and threw a punch, as his fist sped at the man the shotgun's trigger was pulled again and a dozen lead pellets blew Lewis' chest wide open.

"Escumalha die," said that man, apparently this was Portuguese for "Die Scum."

Lewis' eyes looked at the man who then fired his final round of lead that burst Lewis' heart.

Three gunshots sounded and we started sprinting towards the building complex, hopefully Lewis, Jaden, Ollie and Conor were alive, I also prayed that Angelique was here not somewhere else.

Me, Kane, Will, Jack and the stranger Maisie were stood in silence for a few seconds but the echoing blast of gunshots from the building caused a chain reaction between us as we dashed towards the sound of disturbance. Will was in the lead of our single file line as we sprinted and I was towards the back only followed by Maisie who was struggling to keep up, part of me hoped we could lose her for her own safety. Her baby in her arms gazed around with huge brown eyes unaware of the danger it may be running into.

Will burst through a set of fire doors first and rugby tackled the guard who was standing guard there, he gripped his hand over the guard's mouth and knocked him out with a few doses of electricity.

We have emerged into a small square room that seemed to consist of no purpose except as an exit that was never used. There were two doors in the room, one opposite the one we entered through and one to the left.

"Where are we going," Maisie was cut off as Jack covered her mouth with his hand to silence her, from the door to the left we heard a toilet flushing. Everyone stood as still as statues except for Kane who flattened himself against the wall and slid towards the door.

The door handle turned and a balding man in his late 50's came into the room. "Hey don't go in there Roy-," the man spotted us and froze, he slowly reached towards his belt to a large bulge that was more than likely a gun, before his hand reached the weapon Kane brought his gun crashing down on the man's skull, knocking him out for the count.

The man's body collapsed forwards and rolled a few foot to Maisie's feet.

"The man's sleeping George," said Maisie to her baby.

"Let's keep moving," commanded Kane, he shoulder barged his way through the next door with Will and Jack either side off him, as they stepped into this new grey corridor all three of them swept their guns around the area, ready for any ambush, the team worked perfectly together.

I stumbled through behind them with the huge riot shield strapped to my back and a pistol nervously held in hand, every time I moved the shield bashed into the back of my knees, disabling me from running very quickly, not that I was a brilliant runner anyway. At least the shield would protect me from being shot in the back.

The corridor spanned down several hundred metres and consisted of a door on either side every thirty meters. Each door appeared to lead to a separate prison cell as the doors were made out of metal bars.

"Oi what's going on out there!" called a voice from one of the dozen cells, it was unclear which one.

Maisie opened her mouth to speak but once again Jack placed his hand over her to stop her from speaking.

The voice echoed again. "I asked what's happening out there." There was another brief second of bubbling silence then I recognised the voice.

"Jaden?"

"What?" he said, still unaware that we were his rescuers. "Who's that?" His voice was coming from the cell at the very end.

I walked forward until I was outside the cell; Jaden stared at me for a moment then his face broke out in a wide grin.

"I knew I wasn't going to spend the rest of my life here," said Jaden.

"Oh well you may because we're here for Lewis, not you," I said.

Jaden's smile never faltered, he just strode up to me and said blatantly. "Let me out, now."

I fumbled for a second, drawing my gun, then I levelled the black barrel at the lock and pulled the trigger. The bullet snapped the locking mechanism into two pieces like it was a piece of balsa wood and a small hole was left in stone brick wall. I hoped that was the only thing I would have to shoot today.

Jaden tapped the iron barred door making it swing open with great ease. He looked over Jack, Kane, Will and Maisie with an upturned look plastered on his face.

"You made new friends," stated Jaden, his face was as white as paper and his eyes were as purple as plums yet Jaden still managed to pull off his small, smirky smile and the aura that he was the most important person in the room. "What was wrong with your old ones?"

"We need to go," I said, shrugging off Jaden's question. "Where are Lewis and the others?"

"Aren't your new friends going to introduce themselves?" asked Jaden.

"I'm Maisie," said Maisie, the ever vacant look still wandered across her face as she greeted Jaden with a grin.

"I'm Jaden," said Jaden with intrigue playing in his voice. However there was a slight concerned crease in Jaden's forehead, almost as if he knew Maisie.

"Can we go now?" asked Jack, being the ever impatient one as per usual.

No more words were exchanged as the now group of six continued down the seemingly infinite corridor chock full of snaking twists and turns.

Finally we reached another cell that Jaden made us stop at.

The cell was similar to Jaden's except instead of barred doors that could be seen through it was made of reinforced steel that let nothing, not even light, in or out.

"We need to get in here," stated Jaden. He never gave any explanation why but Jack obliged.

Unclipping one of his final four metal tubes from his belt, Jack approached the door and flicked of the lid of the tube he held in his palm. After holding the main button for a second the sickly green fluid that was a corrosive acid jetted from the tube and smothered the door.

Instantly there was a sizzling sound and a hole as wide as a person had burnt away for us to crawl through.

"What's in here?" asked Kane, still curious to whether Jaden could be trusted or not.

Jaden completely ignored Kane's question and crawled through the hole, Will followed next, then me, then Jack, then Maisie and finally Kane. I got stuck for a few seconds trying to crawl through with the bulky riot shield on my back so had to pass it through first.

"This is sick," muttered Jack with awe. The room we were in was an armoury and featured row after row after row of heavy artillery. Crates overflowing with ammunition lined the walls and boxes of grenades were scattered across the floor.

Unfortunately in an armoury is one of the most secure places in any building, so naturally a dozen guards had come to seek refuge here whilst the attack was going on.

"Hey you!" shouted the bravest of the guards as we rounded a corner straight into him.

19

Before the guard spoke another word Jack had raised his pistol to the guard's face and yanked back the trigger. In a mist of blood the man tripped over backwards, knocking over a shelf of machine guns. The other eleven guards had heard this shout however as they came rushing around the shelves, completely surrounding us.

"Drop your weapons!" barked the closest guard; he was aiming a very large shotgun at me. None of us complied and the guard was about to shoot when he noticed the baby that Maisie was clutching like it was made of gold. He seemed confused for a second which gave Will enough time to lob one of the several knives he was in possession of.

The blade embedded itself into the guard's heart as all hell broke loose. The six of us (seven if you counted George) dived to the ground and out of the way of the sudden gunfire.

"What now?" I shouted over the sound of the bullets that were shredding the thin metal shelves, the only things protecting us.

"Fight back Joey!" screamed Jaden, he had snatched the nearest LMG off of the ground and was creeping around the side to advance on the enemy.

Two men ran straight round the corner at us but both fell flat as Kane fired his sniper into one and Jack shot the other in the throat.

Out of the corner of my eye I saw Maisie run away and I chased after. "Wait!" I called. "Stay! It's not safe." Between the shelves I run and caught up to Maisie. She was terrified, her face had gone pale, here heart was going as fast as a jet and her eyes were brimmed with tears. "You can't run," I said you'll be killed."

Across the aisles of shelves Jaden stepped out from behind crates, as silent as the wind and sprayed death upon the guards. Four went down instantly from the rattle of bullets and the other four fled for cover. One of the guards ran right into me and knocked me down.

I grabbed his wrists in a struggle to get him off but the man was two strong, he pinned me down and managed to get his hands around my throat. Maisie stood and watched helplessly as I was throttled by the man.

Suddenly Kane leapt out and swung the butt of his gun. The guard's nose exploded into a torrent of scarlet and he yelped in pain for half a second before Kane fired into the guard's skull.

"Be more careful Joey," Kane said, extending his arm for me to pull myself up on. "I can't lose any more family."

"Thanks," I mumbled ashamed as I pulled myself up. I could have got the man off by shooting him but I had chosen not to.

Behind us Jack had picked up a shotgun and with it blew a hole in another guard's chest. The guard teetered for a second until he fell onto the feet of his comrade who was battling Will.

Will placed his gloved palm over the man's face dispatching thousands of volts into the man's body rendering him immobile. As he collapsed Jaden fired a shot into the man's forehead.

I took a gaze around at the blood and carnage and said. "We need to go find L-." The final guard who had not been dealt with fired a shot directly at me, the lead struck my squarely between the shoulder blades and I collapsed forward as I heard another gunshot that ended the shooters life.

The holes in Lewis closed up extremely quickly and he was back on his feet in a matter of seconds. There were not even any marks left on Lewis' body. The only recognisable difference was that his skin glowed a slight blue. "You shot me," snarled Lewis as his shooter stepped back, utterly bewildered that Lewis was alive. "You shot me," Lewis repeated. His skin was getting increasingly brighter so that the whole corridor was lit up blue.

The shooter span on his heel and broke off into a sprint away from Lewis. He was nowhere near fast enough.

Lewis zipped down the corridor like lightning and grabbed the man's shirt collar as he shot by at the speed of sound.

The two of them crashed into a wall that instantly crumbled at the sheer force. Long cracks ran along the stone floor and then a section of the ceiling that was held up by the wall revealing the red evening sky.

"Why did you shoot me?" growled Lewis to the man that he was holding up by the throat. It was too late however, the impact had killed the man, crushed all his bones so that blood flowed from his mouth. The man's lungs, heart and almost every other organ had collapsed.

Lewis dropped the body onto the ground like it was nothing.

The man who was captive in the cell Lewis had entered yelped and leapt away. He cowered, covering his bloody bruised face, until he noticed who had entered his cell

"Hey Lewis," said Ollie. Lewis had crashed right into and destroyed Ollie's cell.

I blacked out upon impact and my frail body sprawled against a crate of shotguns pellets that tipped over and the thousands of lead balls rolled out like an army of tiny marbles.

Another gunshot echoed through the room quickly followed by the thud of a body with the smell of blood in the air.

My body felt like it had been struck by a train, every muscle and tendon in me ached. This must off mean I was still alive.

My eyelids gradually flicked open so my eyes were greeted by a plain grey sealing as dots floated across my vison. There we definitely people all around me, I could hear their voices yet I couldn't make out what they were saying. I could hear other noises as well, bangs and crashes. Stuck in the scary state of dreams with no escape, unable to move my body. Like I was trapped in my own personal bubble unreachable by the outside world.

The voices persisted and after what felt like an eternity on my back, they grew louder. A lot louder.

"What now!" screamed a voice, one I recognised. "We're surrounded!" The voice was that of Jaden's.

In my peripheral vision I could see his outline to my left, screaming and shooting. Everything was blurry, hostile and painful, but I had some sort of grip on reality.

I opened my mouth to shout Jaden's name but the words wouldn't form themselves. Just a bit of dribble leaked from my mouth.

"Jack I need more ammo!" screamed another voice. This one was Will's. To my right Jack reached into a crate and hurled a magazine full off ammo at Will.

More gunshots when off as my ears popped and my dazed confused self was snapped back into the real world. Sitting up quickly I felt a weight on my chest and realised why I was alive, covering me was the riot shield that I had picked up from the storage warehouse. At the time of the shot the shield had been strapped to my back saving me from the bullets, I was only knocked unconscious due to the sheer force that a bullet delivers.

Kane had spotted me get up and barked orders in my direction. "Joey take a gun, we're surrounded?"

He reached onto a shelf behind him then tossed a fully loaded automatic glock in my direction. The black object skidded across the ground and stopped perfectly between my feet. Picking it up I felt queasy however, I did not want to kill ever again. No one ever gets *everything* they want.

Around me the gunfight continued. Jaden held a pump action shotgun and was firing off rounds at the door straight into anyone brave enough to step through. Kane stood behind me picking off the stragglers that ran with his sniper rifle. Will was stood flat against an iron column as bullets barraged the other side of the support beam that was keeping him alive. Jack loved every second and seemed to be the only one enjoying himself in this chaos and massacre, he was mowing down people left right and centre.

Jack was not watching his back it seemed because I man in clad black riot gear strode up behind the blonde maniac and whacked him on the base of the neck with a metal baton. Jack collapsed like a tonne of bricks.

No one had noticed yet because everyone was too engaged in the ongoing firefight. Except for Maisie who sat in the corner bewildered at the violence.

"Shhh, it's okay," she murmured in George's ear, the baby being the only lucky one completely oblivious to the surrounding bedlam.

Jaden continued firing but the mass numbers of enemies was too great as a dozen men charged. Causing the shelf that acted as a barrier to Jaden to collapse. Trapping the Snowman under a pile of shrapnel and guns.

Will sprinted towards Jaden as another man clad in riot gear slammed into his hips. Both men went tumbling across the room into a wall. Will was the bigger and stronger of the two so managed to get a grip on himself as he shoved the man as hard as he possibly could. The attacker tripped other backwards on himself as Will fired a single round into his skull.

"Ea-," a second attacker grabbed Will by the shoulders then tore him forward. Will stumbled slightly and before he managed to get a hold of himself yet another attacker swung a pipe into Will.

As most of my friends fell I fired a spray of rapid fire bullets across the room towards any advancing enemies. My aim was blinded by rage (not that it was any good before) causing every shot to miss and before I knew it every single bullet in the chamber was gone.

"What do we do?" I bellowed, praying Kane had a suitable answer that didn't end in our deaths.

"There's nothing we can do!" Kane replied. He still fired off random shots but there was nothing he could do against the waves of enemies.

Finally as a dozen men surrounded me in a tight circle more gunfire sounded.

War cries sounded as men fell from the door and more and more bullets sprayed through the room.

In the doorway I saw Lewis, Conor and Ollie, attempting to make their way into the room by force.

Lewis was at the forefront and dove forward knocking a dozen men out of his way as Ollie and Conor flanked him on either side.

"I'm here Joey!" screeched Lewis, sounding like an over excited puppy. He swung his hammer off an arm and knocked an enemy clean over.

Someone advanced on me as Conor shoved through and with his long barrelled SMG fired into the enemies face.

"HUSBAND!" came a cry from the corner. Maisie stood straight up, staring intently at Conor. "You're here." Tears filled her eyes. Maisie looked across the room and saw a man she hadn't seen in a long time, the man she loved. Before she was taken.

Conor spotted his wife and child across the room and froze. The firing stopped for a moment as he was reunited with his wife. Conor dropped his gun and like a raged rhino he barrelled across the room, slamming down as many enemies into the ground at once. He scooped up Maisie in his huge arms and hugged her in a way to show he would never leave her again. Conor then saw his baby son sat up against a crate and hoisted him up. Spilling across his cheeks were streams of tears, tears of pure rejoice of a reunited family once torn apart.

"I'll never leave you," whispered Conor. "Both of you."

Around the joyful reunion Lewis spun on his heels and leapt gracefully from shelf to shelf, blasting away anyone dare step in his path.

I stood up and ran towards Lewis, embracing who was possibly my only friend.

"I'm back Joey," grinned Lewis. "I can't just let you die now. Can I?"

"Actually I'm back," I corrected. "We came here to rescue you."

"Yet in the end I rescued *you*," said Lewis, his smug sense of being better than me around him.

"If you say so."

"I know this is touching," huffed Ollie. "But we have to leave before thirty more men turn up. Plus Jaden and the three over idiots are unconscious, they'll be very dazed."

"So what now?" I asked. I only received a shrug from both Lewis and Ollie whilst Conor was caught up in seeing his wife for the first time in infinity.

I span around and asked Conor a direct question. "How come she's here?" I asked, nodding towards Maisie.

"She was kidnapped," grunted Conor, his face was over Maisie's shoulder so his expression was hidden.

"Why?"

Conor squirmed uncomfortably. "When Jaden was seen with you it was only a matter of time before he contacted me." Conor his tear streaked face. "My wife was taken a few months before; she'd discovered one of Rico's trafficking operations. From there they kidnapped her and my son, tampered with her brain."

"Oh," I muttered.

"It doesn't matter," whispered Conor. "I have here back."

"Guy's," called Lewis. "I can hear noise from down the corridor that thirty people Ollie was talking about may be on the way."

There was a pregnant pause and the sound of footsteps.

"Sorry boys," sounded a feminine voice. "Not thirty people, just little old me."

In the doorway stood a woman, hers hands on her hips and shoulders wide apart. She wore full leather which consisted of leather trousers and a jacket. From on top of her frame were weaves of yellow hair, thin and silky like spider webs.. Behind here blue eyes centred perfectly in her face was hatred. Despite being pretty there was auras about the woman, her features were flawed by a scowl, evil thoughts swarmed through her head that was very obvious upon her face.

"Are you going to stand gawping," growled the woman. "I'm Mortimer, head of this facility. What's your name?"

"It's Lew-," Mortimer drew a pistol from a holster on her thigh and fired a shot into Lewis' forehead. He flipped over backwards and collided into a shelf with a bang.

"Worthless dead weight," snarled Mortimer. "It's not good that you boys attacked my facility, I'll never get promoted if this happens."

I had seen Lewis take a bullet before so I was not too concerned by his predicament. I was worried that a bullet would find its way into my skull.

Ollie raised his pistol towards Mortimer from her left then in a blink he was on the floor. Blood dribbling from the corner of his mouth.

Mortimer had whipped up her foot in a snapping round house kick that had collided with Ollie's face.

"Boys," huffed Mortimer. "Never found a one I haven't wanted to kill."

Mortimer spotted Maisie next to Conor who was cradling George. There was a sudden sparkle in her hateful eyes.

"Girls are fascinating though," said Mortimer, the faintest traces off a smile played on the corners of her mouth. "Girls are better, stronger, we deal with more. Boys are useless. Their only use is to create children but most of them are rubbish at that. Girls can get a job done." Mortimer strode across the room with her chest puffed out in front of her, approaching Maisie.

Conor sidestepped blocking Mortimer's path towards his wife. "You're not touching her," rumbled Conor. George cooed in his arms.

Mortimer swung at Conor a heavy blow, a heavy blow that Conor blocked with his left arm.

He then placed George down next to Maisie as Mortimer stood still.

"How noble," she said sarcastically. "Protecting your love, ah it breaks my hurt." Mortimer struck again and again and again. Conor blocked many blows but Mortimer was too rapid and coordinated so that plenty of jabs made contact with Conor. The giant that he was Conor was struggling and losing energy fast against a combatant he couldn't seem to defeat. Conor swung a punch towards Mortimer's nose that was easily blocked. Conor then raised his knee but Mortimer slapped it down and delivered a quick jab into Conor's torso. As he gasped he brought down a fist that would have crushed Mortimer's skull, would have if she hadn't of stepped backwards and gripped Conor's wrist. From there she pushed downwards and twisted, producing a crack that echoed throughout the room.

Finally Mortimer landed a crushing blow on Conor's throat and he fell to his knees, gasping.

"Never learn," tutted Mortimer. She traipsed around Conor coming face to face with Maisie.

"Hey pretty." Maisie tiptoed backwards as Mortimer advanced. "Conor's very lucky."

With everyone down I realised Mortimer would hurt Maisie and no one was around to stop her. I nosedived forward, trying to get between the two women.

Mortimer's arm whipped out, her flayed palm pulverising my nose. I crumpled down tasting my own blood.

"This is why we girls are better," stated Mortimer. She turned back to Maisie as Conor watched on unable to speak and move. Mortimer circled around the girl who was paralysed with fear and stroked her cheek. "You are *extremely* pretty," grimaced Mortimer. "I hate competition" The gunshot exploded as a perfect hole was formed in Maisie's head that revealed the wall behind. Mortimer had shot Maisie in the head and now smiled at herself. "You just had to break into the facility I'm in charge off," Mortimer gargled. "Maybe now I'll be promoted."

A gargled scream reverberated from Conor and Mortimer stamped her foot down into Conor's face, silencing him.

Maisie teetered on her heels as Mortimer collected George from her arms and tickled his belly. The body dropped with crack in a pool of her own blood.

I reached for Maisie's ankle, and then a foot made everything go black for me.

<u>20</u>

The steady rhythmic beat of the helicopter pounded through the ear drums of every person stood around the stone pedestal. The closest to the helicopter, Dillon Drake, nodded towards the now landing helicopter as Alonzo and One jogged over to the chopper.
 Sand was whipped up by the slowing down blades so Alonzo had to cover his face with his arms, whilst One was fine with his sunglasses.

This helicopter was a particularly large one, washed over in the deepest black and designed to carry up to fifty people.

Alonzo pulled open the door as Mortimer stepped out from the helicopter onto the dessert sand.

"I don't need help you brute," snorted Mortimer to Alonzo. She never looked at him just towards the deep black night and stars that hung above the ancient pyramids.

Alonzo ignored the insult from Mortimer and proceeded to help the helicopters crew drag out the eight men, each tied up with a burlap sack over their heads.

One stood to the side and watched as the men struggled and kicked but were unable to break free from their constricting bonds.

Out of the eight men one of them was not putting up any sort of resistance, and from the rise and fall of their chest One came to the realization that they were unconscious.

This person's burlap sack also had a bullet sized hole where the forehead was, whilst the rest of the sack was stained red with thick blood.

"Mortimer I expect the boys were no trouble," crowed Dillon as the leather clad woman strode over.

"All good," coughed Mortimer. She was clearly repulsed by Dillon Drake but didn't want to show incase her head was torn off. "We had to put a bullet in the tall blonde one's head every couple of minutes though. How do you expect to kill him?"

"I have a way of killing him," smirked Dillon. "Lewis will be dead soon." Dillon felt the satchel hanging on his shoulder making sure the weight of the blade was still there.

"Yes but how could that be achieved?" questioned Mortimer. Dillon seemed irritated by her persistent questions.

"In good time," snapped Dillon. "Now step aside and shut up."

In her head Mortimer imagined snapping Dillon's neck then popping his head, yet she wouldn't be able to get two steps before Dillon tore her limb from limb.

Laid out on the large pedestals were two people side by side. On the right was Rico Angel, sniveling and weeping.

"I can't die," he croaked. "I'm too important."

On the left lay Angelique, bruised and battered but not crying, she had come to terms with her death and had not resorted to begging like the heartless fool beside her.

Neither of them could see what was going on around as they were bound from their toes to their neck in heavy ropes.

Looming over the pair stood The Executioner, wielding her axe over her shoulder as per usual, minutes away from killing.

I coughed and splattered as sand flowed into my mouth. I was being dragged by my ankles across scorching hot sand. The thousands of granules of sand flowed up my nose and into my mouth causing me to choke.

Two hands had a firm grip on my ankles and were pulling me towards the source of a lot of noise. After being knocked unconscious once again, I was sensing a pattern, we were taken onto a helicopter. There was a very long helicopter journey that consisted of only the sound of the helicopters blades and a gunshot every few minutes. We had all been blinded by the bags over our heads.

I could hear several ongoing conversations but the sound of sand shifting and a ringing in my ears rendered words inaudible.

My brain was still working as hard as possible to comprehend the events that had happened prior to me blacking out. I remembered that woman Mortimer knocking most of us unconscious and shooting Lewis. Then shooting Maisie....

"Do I just chuck him with the others?" grunted a gruff voice to my left.

"No," sounded a female to my right. "Dillon wants him and the blonde boy over by the pedestal for the ritual."

"Okay I'll bring him over," said the man. "You bring the other."

I felt myself shift direction then I was being dragged the other way.

"I'll kill you all!" screamed Lewis. His reassuring manic voice echoed out across the desert sand making me smile.

Then a gunshot sounded and Lewis was hushed, for the moment at least.

The smell of burning blew along on the wind and forced itself into my nostrils. Specks of ashes and dust drifted across the Egyptian plains.

I was dragged for a few more seconds then was stationary.

"Don't make any trouble Joey," said the man with the gruff voice. I seemed to recognize his voice but I could barely make out his words.

Suddenly a pain shot through my gut like I had been hit by a bullet train as my captor landed a kick against me.

"Don't make any trouble or Dillon will do you worse to you." The burlap sack was lifted from my face and I was confronted by the hulking frame of Alonzo.

He turned his back on me then walked towards a colossal campfire that had been built up here in the eternal darkness of the night. I just lay, curled in a ball, clutching my stomach.

Where I lay was on top of a sand dune, next to a stone pedestal. Around me spanned darkness as far as the eye could see and the only light was cast by the campfire that flickered across the faces of thirty people.

Closest to the campfire was One, staring intently into the flames with his expression neutral as ever and his eyes hidden behind his shades. To his left extremely close was a figure hidden under an oversized hood that covered their entire face.

Another dozen men and a few women sat nervously around the flames, unsure what to do. None of them were certain about what was going to happen in the next hour.

Behind the fire Mortimer stood with another man, she was scowling at him and speaking. I couldn't hear her words but by the expression on her face I could tell they weren't happy words.

"Joey?" whispered someone to my left. A voice I certainly recognized. "Is that you?"

Next to me, tied to the pedestal, was Angelique.

"Angelique," I squealed. "You're here!"

"Did you come here for me?" she asked. Her soft feminine was voice playing with my emotions as per usual.

"Actually I went to Portugal looking for you," I admitted. "But I got kidnapped and ended up here."

"Why are we here?" Angelique asked. "I heard something about a ritual."

"I don't know." I sat up and was going to reach round and help Angelique when I realized that my hands were bound by rope.

"I don't think there's much we can do."

"Are you sure Joey," croaked Rico. The soulless man was tied next to Angelique and had been listening in on our conversation. "You're smart Joey, get us out somehow," he sniveled.

"Even if I could get out I'd leave you here to rot," I snarled, hatred for Rico boiling inside me. "I wouldn't save you if my life depended on it.

Rico turned his head so it was faced towards me even though his vision was blocked by the back of Angelique's head.

"Rot in hell Joey Tyler," thundered Rico, his voice rasping. "I gave you a job, a home, a new life. This is how you repay me? Joey, you deserve everything that's coming to you and more. A decent person would forgive me after the hospitality I gave you."

"Hell will freeze over when I forgive you," I replied. "And that's exactly where you're going after today. If someone else doesn't kill you I will." In my stomach I knew that I would not have the capability to murder Rico but I hoped somebody else would after the atrocities he had committed.

"Joey Tyler when I break free I will personally-," Angelique snapped her head backwards and cracked it against Rico's nose rendering him mute.

"Thanks," I huffed.

"I've wanted to do that the entire time I've worked at W.S.I," grinned Angelique, the impending doom seemingly escaping her mind. "Me too."

There were a few shouts and a single gunshot as Lewis woke up again and had to be put down by another bullet.

Angelique reached down a gripped my hand as I leant back against the stone pedestal and held hers. We sat like this in unbroken silence until the sun rose in the morning, just holding each other.

As the golden orb of a sun crept over the saffron sand dunes and cast a streak of light across the horizon that ended squarely on the pedestal, Dillon walked over.

"Mr Tyler," he called. Angelique and I looked over towards our possible to be killer, not separating our hands. "This isn't personal," Dillon explained. "I have a mission to fulfill and it just so happens you have to be killed. I'm a huge fan of your work though." Dillon smirked and made a hand gesture indicating for his men to walk over.

Mortimer, One, Alonzo and four other men marched over, each dragging a bound up person behind them.

"Mortimer kill the troublesome one again," barked Dillon. Mortimer took great pleasure of removing the burlap sack from the face of her man to reveal Lewis with a rapid healing hole in his head. She then drew her pistol out of its holster and fired into Lewis' head for the umpteenth time today.

"I'll never get tired of that," stated Mortimer coldly.

"The rest of you reveal our guests," Dillon ordered. The other six men removed the face covers on their captives revealing my friends. Each on their knees in a row, bloody and bruised, were Kane, Will, Jack, Conor, Jaden and Ollie.

"Who's going to die first?"

The executioner stood alone a hundred meters from the now dying campfire; she was mesmerized by the size and power of the great Sphinx that sat before her. The millennium old creature apparently held a dark secret. Something ancient and evil was held deep within the snow. According to Dillon.

Whatever was in the Sphinx, Dillon desperately wanted it out now. The executioner did not want to kill these people; she didn't want to kill anyone really. Maybe at the start but not anymore.

If Dillon managed to set free the creature hidden inside the Sphinx then all hell would rain upon the Earth.

Horrible thoughts swarmed through Conor's mind, ideas to pull Mortimer apart limb for limb and tear her skin off. He wanted to grab the dumb bitch by the throat and repeatedly kick her in her face. She had killed Conor's wife, the fate of his son, George, was still unknown. Mortimer may have killed George or spared him. However it was unlikely he was spared because Mortimer had travelled straight here to Egypt and George wasn't here. Conor swore to himself that eventually he would avenge his wife. Mortimer just stood unfazed behind Conor; reveling over the pain she had caused the pain and looking forward to when all of these men would be dead.

Alonzo strode over to me, Angelique and Rico. He drew a jagged rusty blade from a sheath onto his thigh. For half a second I was worried that Alonzo was going to kill us right now. Instead he severed the ropes that bound Rico and Angelique to the stone pedestal.
"Move!" he bellowed then grabbed Rico by his dirty, bloodied collar and threw the old man down into the sand where he rolled over a few meters. Angelique didn't need to be shoved, instead she tried to stand herself up but her legs were too weak to stand after the previous few days and she collapsed down onto the dunes.
I reached over to help her but instead Alonzo swung his hammer arm into my chest flinging me back into the ground.
Mortimer stood tall behind me and sniggered as I crashed down.

"Silence Mortimer!" called Dillon. "We must begin."

The thirty or so men and women working for Rico gathered around Dillon including Alonzo, Mortimer, One and The Executioner.
"Alonzo bring the needed ones to our master!" shouted Dillon.

Alonzo gripped Angelique's right arm and dragged her across the sand towards the great sphinx. Mortimer followed by dragging Rico towards the monument. Next One marched up behind and jammed his pistol into my spine, indicating that I should follow the others.
The rest of Dillon's group followed behind us and at the very back Dillon dragged Lewis' unmoving body.
Kane, Jaden, Jack, Will, Conor and Ollie were left back by the helicopter, still tied up and blind folded.

In the back of Dillon's a voice echoed. *"You will be greatly rewarded for this Mr Drake."*
The voice was like a combination of nails on a chalkboard and a snake's hiss, it sent a sharp

chill down Dillon's spine yet he smiled. Dillon had nearly completed his task, in the new world order Dillon would be near the top.

"What are you doing?" said Angelique. Alonzo ignored here a kept dragging her forward. Then he propelled her backwards with great force where she crashed into the stone of the sphinx. Mortimer followed up by shoving Rico down next to Angelique.
 One did not shove me, instead he gave me the opportunity to sit down myself but before I got the chance to I was shoved down my Mortimer. "Bitch," I muttered as I clattered into the dust.
 "I will hurt you!" snarled Mortimer, apparently hearing my curse.

 Dillon drew a scrap of her paper from his pocket and started to read.

To find The Monster that you seek,
Travel to a known antique,
Through a thriving yet dead land,
Dominated by time and sand,
"This is clearly the sphinx in ancient Egypt," stated Dillon.
To bring the beast from the his constricting pool,

Take the soul of someone cruel,
"Rico of course."
If you don't wish to be the beasts eat,
Find the soul of someone sweet,
"And that is why we have Angelique," explained Dillon.
Finally you'll need the key,
Locked away for eternity,
Until you kill its second part,
Just be warned he is smart,
"The key is you Joey Tyler!" exclaimed Dillon. This brought a string of boys from the thirty surrounding men and women. "We must kill Lewis for this to work!"

"How?" I asked. My curiosity had been piqued. "Bullets won't stop Lewis."

"I have a way," answered Dillon, he opened his Jacket and drew a knife. The blade was rather long and it glowed blue. "This will kill your friend."

I had no idea if the blade would work but it radiated a sense around it of power.

"Now to begin the ritual Lewis must be killed!"

As the sun reached its peak in the sky and a blistering hot heat pelted down on the heads of every man and woman, Dillon approached Lewis' body.

Small pockets of sand swirled around the Sphinx as Dillon grabbed Lewis' limp frame and yanked him up.

"I told Joey this wasn't personal," whispered Dillon. "But I do hate you Lewis." Dillon raised his arm then plunged his blade into Lewis' heart in a spurt of sticky blood.....

_**21**_

Jaden, Kane, Jack, Ollie, Will and Conor were still bound up and lined up in that order. Through vigorous shaking Jaden had managed to remove the blindfold from his face.

"Kane can I ask you a favour?" asked Jaden, menace in his voice.

"Is this really the time Snow?" snapped Kane.

"This could get us out of here," chirped Jaden.

"It's not very pleasant though."

"What is it?" huffed Kane.

"Reach down the back of my shorts," said Jaden. "I have a flick knife down there. It could cut our ropes. I would reach down there but my bounds won't let me reach."

"Nope!" said Kane. "No way!"

"Just do it Kane," Jack called out.

"Yeah we need to escape," agreed Will.

"I can't do that though," said Kane. "It's gross; I have no idea where he's been."

"We have to get out," muttered Ollie. Conor was silent.

"Just grab the knife Kane."

"Why can't any of you do it?" moaned Kane.

"You are closest," shrugged Jaden. "Just get to it."

Kane rolled over in the sand, turned around and reached.

"Kane?" said Jaden.

"This is not the time," grunted Kane, searching for the blade.

"I forgot," stated Jaden.

"What?" said Kane, unable to find a knife, moving away.

"The knife is in my sock."

As Kane sustained an expression that looked like he wanted to murder Jaden, the others couldn't help but stifle a laugh. All except for Conor, Conor was silent and motionless.

Nothing happened. Lewis remained unmoving still and the entirety of everyone was stone silent.

Lewis remained unmoving on the ground in a gradually growing pool of his own blood. His chest stab wound wasn't healing.

"He's not dead," I thought in my head. "He can't be!" I screamed inside my mind.

Nothing could kill Lewis, yet he lay unmoving, not healing.

"Lewis is dead," said Dillon. "We now continue."

The crowd stood in stunned silence, as still as Lewis' body, whilst Dillon approached Rico.

"Mr Tyler. Did you know that this knife was specially made by the Egyptians to kill my master?" asked Dillon. "They made it about the same time that my master was trapped in here." Dillon patted the paw of the stone sphinx that towered above everyone. "One touch of the blade would even someone with my immense power; possibly it would even kill the beast in here."

Dillon got down onto his knees so he was level with the slumped Rico.

"You are a horrible man Rico," snarled Dillon. "Committing acts of heinous crimes, just for a profit. You are pathetic."

"Please spare me," sniveled Rico. "I can't die. I'll pay you anything I can."

"You don't really learn," said Dillon. "Do you?"

I wasn't paying attention when Dillon arched his arm and thrust the blade into Rico's throat. Blood splatted out across in patches onto the yellow stone bricks and specks of blood flicked over Angelique's face and clothes. This is the moment I had known was coming for a long time, Rico's crimes had caught up on him and now he was paying. A better fate than he deserved but still paying.

I was instead focused on Lewis' body as Rico slipped down leaving a streak of blood behind him. In my head I prayed that Lewis would wake up. Lewis had saved my life multiple times, he was my guardian angel. I was a frail, stupid sheep and he had been a shepherd. It had only been a week but after losing everything else I had become attached to Lewis .

"Now what?" asked Mortimer, growing impatient by the time being taken for the ritual? "Patience Mortimer!" bellowed Dillon.

"Are you going to kill the blonde bitch now?" asked Mortimer.

"You're lucky I'm in a good mood Mortimer," said Dillon. "The blood of the key and the blood of a truly evil man have been spilled on the sphinx. Once the blood of the innocent kill has been spilled, my master will awaken."

"So that's a yes?"

"Continue like this and I'll shoot you," growled Dillon.

Dillon advanced now towards Angelique.

"Now the last to die then," Dillon smiled. "It's an honor; your sacrifice will lead to a new world order."

"Don't do this," I pleaded. "You don't have to." I dived forward between Dillon and Angelique then Dillon wedged his foot under my chest and flipped me over four feet back.

"I'm not killing this one," stated Dillon. "I have no vendetta against her; I did against Rico and Lewis. My executioner will kill this one."

The executioner stumbled forward out of the crowd, her axe hung over her right shoulder.

"Decapitate her," ordered Dillon.

The Executioner took a few steps forward, her palms were sweaty, hers knees were weak and her arms were heavy. The axe sat awkwardly as she gripped it in her hands, ready to swing.

She raised the axe up above her head, preparing to bring it crashing down. I watched in horror as she arched her arms downwards bringing the axe towards the ground.

The metal blade smacked down into the sand next to Angelique's head.

"I can't do it," sniffed The Executioner. "I've killed before. Never anyone innocent though. I just can't do this anymore."

Dillon didn't move a muscle; instead Alonzo stepped forward from the crowd and fired a shot into the executioner's leg. Her knee cap exploded in a pop of red blood and she collapsed into a heap with a cry of pain.

One did nothing as she bled in the sand but felt sympathy for the woman, she was the lone person One had even remotely liked and she was bleeding into the sand. One didn't want to do this no more, he wanted to leave, leave Alonzo and Dillon. Yet he stood still.

"I'll kill her myself then," sighed Dillon. "It's a shame. I liked you executioner. You say boys are useless but girls can be just as much of a hindrance Mortimer."

Mortimer cursed the man under her breath but was ignored by everyone.

Dillon drew his knife for the final time. "I have to kill everyone myself."

"Not everyone," said Lewis. "I'll be the one to kill you."

22

The hole in Lewis' heart and healed and the wound was gone. Then he shot forward faster than my brain could comprehend and gripped Dillon by the waist.

Both Lewis and Dillon skidded across the desert floor and brushed over the top of a sand dune. Millions of specks of dust scattered outwards in a puff.

They continued to shoot across the horizon, landing hammering blows on each other's faces and torsos that would kill a normal human. The too grabbled at the other ones body as they crashed straight the nearest pyramid. Stone exploded outwards and rubble rolled down the steps like an avalanche as they burst out of the pyramids other side.

Lewis gripped his hand right hand onto Dillon's face and forced his fingers into Dillon's empty eye socket, clawing at the nerves and vessels inside, drawing a stream of thick red blood.

Dillon screamed and clutched Lewis' arm, he jerked his arm out of the socket as Lewis' humerus bone snapped in two leaving his arm limp and frail.

As the two of them crashed into the ground Lewis' arm healed and he punched Dillon straight in the jaw dislocating it.

Lewis stood up and from the sand and spat out a tooth that would soon grow back. He raised his fists to protect himself but Dillon's arm swiped through the fists, shattering all of the bones in each hand, and then proceeded to grip Lewis by the waist and shoot off again.

Everyone was so focused on the ongoing battle that no one had noticed that the now free Kane, Will, Jack, Jaden, Conor and Ollie had stolen weapons from the chopper and had surrounded Dillon's men and women.

Each was fifty meters back, laying the sand in a circle around everyone.

"Fire!" shouted Kane over the sound of the pyramid that Dillon and Lewis had leapt through collapsing.

"Who put him in charge?" complained Jaden, when no response came he pulled his trigger like the rest of the group.

A hail of bullets rattled towards the crowd from every direction, mowing down the gang Dillon had gathered to witness the ritual.

Ollie squeezed his eyes tight as he fired; hoping not to hit anyone as the killing machine in his hands recoiled, battering his shoulder.

Most people fled as fast as they could, only to be gunned down hastily.

The few who did not panic in the mass hysteria were Alonzo, Mortimer and One. The executioner also did not run but only because the ability to walk had been snatched from her.

One dived for cover behind the stone pedestal that Rico and Angelique had been held on. He fired off a few shots towards the direction of Conor but none met their target.

Mortimer dropped into the sand and unclipped a spare Uzi she kept hanging from her belt. She started to crawl towards where Kane was firing off sniper rounds from.

Finally Alonzo collected the machine gun from a fallen comrade that Will had struck down and then flattened himself against the Sphinx, proceeding around the stone giant towards Jack.

Angelique and I had to stay incredibly still, hoping we would not be mistaken for an enemy.

I could have made a dash for it but I stayed with Angelique who was still bound to the sphinx's mighty paw.

"Stay still!" I shouted over the gunfire as a barrage of bullets clattered against the sandstone that Alonzo was pressed against, a few inches from my head!

Alonzo ducked out from his cover for a half a second a sprayed a few dozen random shots towards the closest shooter. Whoever the shooter was, it appeared to be Ollie, and they stopped firing.

Mortimer had crawled the distance towards where Kane was shooting from; she aimed her Uzi up in line with his head, ready to spray off a round.

However Kane spotted her and ducked a split second before a hundred bullets tore apart where his head had been.

Kane rolled in the sand as more shots shredded the ground next to him. Mortimer pulled the trigger again only to hear the unsatisfying sound of an empty clip.

"Have to kill him the old fashioned way," huffed Mortimer. She ditched the gun in the sand and sprinted up the sand dune towards Kane.

He pulled back the catch on his gun so he could fire another shot but before Kane got his finger upon the trigger Mortimer smashed into him.

The pair hit the ground with a thump as Mortimer gripped her hands around Kane's throat, jamming her thumbs down on his windpipe.

Kane choked and struggled then grabbed Mortimer's hair. He yanked as hard as he could and his hand came away with a bunch of bloody blonde hair. Mortimer screamed in pain and released her grip from Kane's throat; she laid her hand on the bloody patch on her head.

"You stupid boy!" snarled Mortimer. "You messed up my hair!" Mortimer dived at Kane once again as he lunged forward with the sniper held forward. Mortimer's head cracked against the guns' barrel, collapsing backwards, down the dune.

Kane left her unconscious on the ground and sprinted towards me and Angelique.

Jack was once again having too much fun. A man turned towards him with a pistol and Jack dropped into the sand, firing bullets into the man's chest. He had had his tubes of explosive goo confiscated by Mortimer back in Portugal but sometimes guns were just as fun.

He aimed his sights again, went to squeeze the trigger. Then a huge arm wrapped around his throat and flipped him across a set of shoulders. Alonzo stood over him grinning from ear to, well where his other should have been. Jack instantly spotted the gun in Alonzo's hand and fired. Bullets tore through cartilage and bone that made up Alonzo's left hand as he screamed and gripped it. Blood gushed through his fingers and Alonzo snarled at Jack. As the huge brute knelt in the sand Jack stood and smiled, happy with himself for bringing the tower of a man down. Jack's victory was short-lived as Alonzo rose from the ground and head butted Jack, the small blonde boy stepped back and winced as a thin trail of blood ran from his nose and a blinding dizziness pounded his brain.

"I-is that all you've got," stuttered Jack. Alonzo followed up by stamping on Jack's toe and elbowing him in the chest. Jack collapsed and Alonzo stood over him.

"Pathetic," Alonzo growled. Before he had the chance to finish Jack off a cry echoed. A hundred meters away Dillon called out, he shouted to fall back and Alonzo complied. He ran away from the battle and left Jack who just got back to his feet.

"Run away!" shouted Jack. "I win!"

Will dashed around the edge of the gunfire and towards the helicopter like Kane had instructed him to do after most of the enemies had been killed. He slid open the door into the helicopter and stepped into the vast cockpit. Will started up the engine and waited for the others to arrive.

All of a sudden One dived through the helicopter's open door and grabbed Will's collar. One yanked him backwards and tried to pull Will out. One was faster and more skilled than his opponent but Will was far stronger and managed to drag One into the cockpit. From there he punched One squarely in the nose. As a thin trail of red flowed from One's face Will flipped him over the back off the pilot's seat and into the cargo carrying section of the helicopter. One smacked against the cold metal floor but sprung back up instantly, ready to fight. Will threw a punch that was meant to break One's nose. Instead One dropped down low and kicked Will's ankles out from underneath him.

Will crumpled down like a tonne of bricks and banged against the ground.

On the ground with One stood over him Will slapped with fist against the red button on the wall to his right. The hangar doors to the helicopter spread open as Will pumped his legs forward into One's chest. He went tumbling out of the helicopter's back as Will marched out following him.

One snapped up from the ground again, once again ready to fight.

"Can you just stay down," growled Will. He threw another punch at One which was easily dodged. Then another, then another. One still easily dodged every blow and landed an elbow underneath Will's rib. Will doubled over as the wind was knocked from him and One cracked down a fist on the back of Will's neck. He dropped to the ground as One thundered a quick knee into Will's chin and a fist into Will's neck.

As One stood over him, he drew a knife from the inside of his Jacket, a predator ready to strike the prey.

All of a sudden One collapsed unconscious into the sand. Ollie stood behind him clutching his gun which he had slapped into One's temple.

"Thanks," gasped Will as Ollie offered him a hand to pull himself up on.

Ollie ran into the helicopter's cargo storage as Will slid into the pilot's seat, waiting for the others.

Lewis and Dillon continued to battle, shattering bones and tearing muscles. Each healed faster and faster but a victor did not seem likely soon. Dillon thumped his fist into Lewis' chest, cracking all of the ribs near the impact. However all of the bones instantly healed and Lewis struck Dillon's solar plexus with his elbow.

They continued to brawl in the air but neither was relenting and both could continue this for days more.

Jack, Jaden and Conor all jogged towards me to survey the damage off their firing.

Conor waded through the dozen bodies around me whilst Jaden and Jack approached me and Angelique.

"Are you alright?" asked Jaden. "I didn't shoot you did I?"

"I'm f-." Jaden cut me off as he noticed Angelique.

"Hey babe," Jaden said with a wink. "I came here just to save you."

"You and seven other people," scowled Angelique.

"But mainly me."

Angelique ignored Jaden and turned to Jack. "Will you cut us loose short stack?" she asked. Jack stepped forward, ignoring the insult aimed at his short stature, and with a large knife he recovered from a body he slashed through Angelique's bounds then the rope wrapped round my wrists.

"Thanks," I muttered, rubbing my sore wrists.

"What happened to wrinkles?" asked Jaden, inspecting Rico's bled out body. The gash in his neck was wide enough to fit your hand in and had leaked all of the blood in Rico's frail body.

"Part of Dillon's ritual," I explained.

"Ritual?" said Jack.

"He was doing something where he had to kill Lewis, Rico and Angelique to bring back some old guy."

"I'll just pretend I know what that mean," said Jack.

Conor had gone around all of the bodies making sure were really dead and looped back to us.

"We should return back to the meeting point and escape," said Conor. He didn't look anyone in the eyes, alternatively his eyes just wandered across the mammoth pyramids that lined the horizon. Conor had lost everything in a matter of a few minutes and now was empty inside. His wife was dead and his son missing. Now Conor was left to tag along with Jaden and six other almost complete strangers.

"Meeting point?" I asked.

"We agreed to get back to the chopper after we rescued you and Angelique," answered Jaden.

"What about rescuing Lewis?"

"We saw him die," said Jack.

"A knife wouldn't kill him," I scoffed. "He's up there." I pointed towards the closest pyramid where a cloud of dust was being whipped up by two figures sealed in combat.

Upon the pyramid Lewis bombarded his fist upon Dillon's stomach as he drooped down. Dillon stamped his foot that split the stone in two like it was made of butter. Both tumbled into a small chamber inside the pyramid, left untouched for centuries. Dillon prepared to strike Lewis again until he dropped as something echoed inside him.

"You have failed me!" roared a voice like thunder in the base off Dillon's skull. "Stop wasting your time fighting and bring me back!" The voice that bounced throughout Dillon's mind scraped down his soul like nails on a chalkboard and a sensation that felt like a thousand ice cold knifes piercing his brain made Dillon leap away from Lewis. He crashed through the stone wall and proceeded to retreat from the desert as fast as the human eye could comprehend.

As Dillon skimmed across the boiling sand at swift speeds the voice continued to echo inside his head. From here all the way on the journey back to London.

"You failed me! I will punish you! You failed me! I will punish you!"

22

Lewis pulled himself out of the pyramid instead of pursuing Dillon and proceeded towards where I was.

"I'm back," grinned Lewis. "Praise me now."
"We have to leave," I said. "And no, I won't praise you."
"Fine then don't," murmured Lewis. "I'm sure everyone else will."
After no one praised Lewis he just sulked in silence and followed us back to the helicopter.
We were greeted by Kane, Will and Ollie as we all loaded into the back.
I noticed One's unconscious body slumped a few feet away but ignored it.

"Where to then everyone?" asked Will from the pilot's seat with the joystick in hand.

Out of the nine people in the helicopter no one knew where to go or what to do now. We had all lost everything in the world and half of us were thought to be dead to the world.

We had stopped Dillon's ritual; his master would stay in the sphinx, for now. Dillon's troops had been scattered or shot and Rico was dead.

Yet Dillon was still out there, as long as the one-eyed man still lived he would try to find a way to bring back his master. He would find a way to kill Lewis. I knew Lewis couldn't die, I had witnessed that multiple times yet part of me felt that wasn't definite. Everyone had to die one day.

"Let's just get far away," suggested Ollie and he was answered by a chorus and nods and yes'.

Will pushed down on the joystick and steadily the helicopter rose up into the sky then away from the desert. It flew over the city of Cairo with a steady beat as hundreds of merchants, beggars and millionaires gazed up at us. Unaware of the massacre that had just happened.

As the helicopter neared the red sea the room was filled with speech.

Angelique introduced herself to Jack as they talked about life before. Ollie and Jaden were locked in a conversation about who would win in an arm wrestle whilst neither was willing to test that and up front Kane and Will chatted casually about a memory they shared from long ago. Conor didn't want to engage in conversation and just eyed the sea below.

After a while I turned my head towards Lewis.

"You owe me an explanation about now," I said.

"What?" yawned Lewis.

"You have to tell me everything. How was you in my locket? How did you know me? Why can't you die? Why would you help me?"

"I shouldn't be telling you why."

"I have a right to know."

"I will tell you."

"When though?"

"Do you want to know?" asked Lewis

"More than anything."

"Okay then. Let me explain everything." said Lewis.

The helicopter glided over the ocean, unaware of its destination because everyone in the helicopter had non home to go to. Dillon had to continue pursuing us, he wouldn't relent.

Dillon had another idea, a way to return his master. The same thing that wouldn't allow Lewis to die could cause his death; allow his master a passage to our world. All would be done in time. Everything would fall into place. Today had been a setback, but tomorrow would be a new day, tomorrow Dillon's last resort would come into play. All the power he needed, all of the power in the world. Concealed in Joey Tyler's locket.

To be continued......

Printed in Great Britain
by Amazon.co.uk, Ltd.,
Marston Gate.